TWO FOR A PENNY

A Post-war Childhood

E L Campbell

ATHENA PRESS
LONDON

TWO FOR A PENNY
A Post-war Childhood
Copyright © E L Campbell 2005

All Rights Reserved

ISBN 1 84401 501 7

First Published 2005 by
ATHENA PRESS
Queen's House, 2 Holly Road
Twickenham TW1 4EG
United Kingdom

Printed for Athena Press

TWO FOR A PENNY

A Post-war Childhood

To Mam and Dad
with love and thanks for my childhood.

Contents

The Early Years

Both infant classes were brought together in the larger of the two rooms, the one which was used as the classroom for the older children. There was much excited chatter among the children because this was an unusual event and it made a change from their routine – a chance for everyone to mingle and to chat together. The high spirits didn't last for long. The sudden appearance in their midst of the Headteacher, Miss Nairn, and the uncompromising presence she brought with her effectively quelled all exuberance.

"Now children, you have been gathered together because I have some very grave news to tell you concerning our King," she intoned. As the children struggled with the meaning of "grave news", she went on: "His Majesty King George, who has been ill for a long time, has passed away. He is reported to have died peacefully in his sleep at Sandringham House."

While the expressions on the young faces indicated that they were still digesting the import of her announcement, Miss Nairn continued: "We will now say prayers for the soul of King George and for all the royal family, especially Queen Elizabeth, his wife."

With practised concentration, little faces screwed up with eyes tight shut and palms joined in prayer. Together, children and teachers alike recited Our Father, Hail Mary, Glory Be and Eternal Rest, with Miss Nairn reading out the Memorare. They listened dutifully as she followed the profound news with the information that Princess Elizabeth was returning from her holiday in East Africa to be with the rest of the family of the deceased King, her father, who had died aged only fifty-six.

Playtime immediately followed. It was thought that perhaps the children needed some emotional release. They were somewhat frustrated in this, however, as it was steadily drizzling outside and they had to content themselves with playing indoors.

When Shirley Calvert came to the infant gate to collect Tommy, she rather unnecessarily gave him the same news as she had heard in the juniors.

"I know, Miss Nairn told us," he replied. "What do we do without a King?"

"Well, there'll be another one I expect," said Shirley, although she wasn't sure of the procedure herself.

It would be some time later when such matters of state became evident to them.

What was beginning to form a pattern of sorts was the fact that events of some profound historical significance to his nation were occurring at fairly frequent intervals in young Tommy's development. After all, he was born in May 1945 – the very month that the Nazi war machine finally succumbed to the overwhelming advance of the Allies.

Tommy left the infants that summer to make the short journey but the huge transition to the junior school. From the squat prefabricated structure that comprised the Infant School, Tommy and his classmates transferred to the huge stone building across the far side of the junior playground. It was made more massive both in fact and in their imaginations because the school lay underneath the parish church, which itself had a steep tiled roof. Together they blotted out half the sky in that direction.

It wasn't long before Tommy settled into life in the juniors. He had ability – at least compared to many of his peers, a considerable number of whom struggled to read adequately and were even less numerate. This was no reflection on the efforts and skill of Miss Nairn and her colleagues, but more an indication of the deprived backgrounds of many of their pupils. Miss Nairn had, after all, taught Tommy to read quite well, which wasn't an easily accomplished feat.

In these early post-war years, rationing was still rife and the living standard of the average family in Nelson was still quite spartan. In this respect, the Calverts were comparatively comfortable, if only through the sweated labour of Mrs as well as Mr Calvert. Having lived through the war with considerable family disruption, they were determined to better themselves, perhaps more so than many in Nelson.

They had migrated from Liverpool soon after the war, as Mr Calvert had found work in the local sweet factory. His wife gained employment in the weaving sheds – rewarding but tiring work for a housewife with a family to raise.

Nelson was so very different from the metropolis of Merseyside as to be almost an alien environment. Among the early acquaintances of the Calverts in their new home were Scots and Geordies, with whom they probably found a kindred spirit. It would be several years before the friendly folk of East Lancashire would take fully to anyone not born and bred in the area.

It was easier for Mr Calvert, working as he did in a factory environment which contained an assortment of incoming labour from other regions and even from abroad, most notably Poland.

Mrs Calvert, on the other hand, had to win over the local women on the adjacent looms to hers; first of all overcoming their prejudice born of fear at the threat to their labour, and secondly managing to get them to help her induction into the specialised world of the weaving sorority. This would include mastering the art of lip-reading.

Now that Tommy was settled in to the junior department of St Joseph's, and his older sister fully acclimatised, the Calverts could rightly take their place in Nelson society as locals and not incomers.

Tommy was about to make further progress along the road of acceptance. It was the year of his first Sacraments. This would involve the serious business of him becoming accountable for his own actions in the eyes of the Church. He was reaching the age of responsibility. This would be officially tested when, after much tuition and preparation, he and his classmates made their first Confession. This was a necessary prelude to receiving Communion.

The fact that they had to undergo this ritual at the hands of Father Lister did nothing to make the task any more palatable. But somehow, Tommy and the others survived the ordeal of the dark and dusty confessional where they had to admit their transgressions to a gloomy grille surrounded by a curtain and set into the partition.

On the other side of the partition loomed the shadowy profile of the formidable priest. Surely he would be deeply shocked at the evil revelations of these young reprobates? However, a blessing followed by a few Hail Marys seemed to do the trick, and anyway, he had no way of telling which child was guilty of which misdemeanours, had he?

However much instruction was given to the young "acolytes" in order to get them ready for their special Mass, nothing could prepare them for the strange taste and consistency of the Communion wafer. By the end of the service, Tommy was beginning to perspire from the combined effect of the shirt and tie that he wore and the heat from the many candles, one of which each child had to grip between clenched and sweaty palms as they formed a procession to walk between the lines of pews and out of the church.

At least the Communion breakfast served in the school classroom was adequate compensation, though why it was termed a breakfast when it took place in the afternoon and there was no sign of any cereals caused no little confusion among the recipients. There was, however, an abundance of paste sandwiches, home-baked cupcakes and jelly, all liberally washed down with beakers of orange squash.

Tommy was to further cement his association with the parish by being "volunteered" to train as an altar boy. He seemed to accept this honour with stoicism, subjecting himself to many sessions of apprenticeship. These involved learning the prayer responses in Latin with the help of Mr Cooper, who seemed so old that Latin may have been the tongue of his schooldays.

It would be some time before Tommy would be given a position of responsibility on the altar. Until then he was there just to make up the numbers and add to the grandeur of the occasion when a string of vestmented altar servers preceded Father Lister as he emerged from the sacristy to begin the Sunday Mass.

The summer term of Tommy's first year in the juniors witnessed even more profound events. There was the news that the world's highest mountain had been conquered (not just climbed) by a British expedition. The fact that Edmund Hilary was a New Zealander and Tensing Norgay a Sherpa did not lessen the impact of the nation's joy.

Patriotic celebrations reached a peak when the Princess Elizabeth was crowned as the new Head of State. The coronation ceremony in Westminster Abbey on June 6th, though followed only on the radio by the majority of folk in Nelson, gave rise to a fervour of pride.

The main impact on Tommy was the local celebration arranged by the municipal council dignitaries to mark the occasion. All the junior children at St Joseph's were lined up in the yard to meet the mayor. He in turn presented each child with a glass beaker. This was painted blue, had a picture of the new Queen on the side and contained a bag of sweets. The beaker lasted considerably longer than did its contents.

The new queen was left to reign in peace while Tommy resumed normal service, continuing his education not just in school but on almost every occasion he played around the streets of home with his growing circle of friends.

There was Peter, who attended the same school as Tommy and occasionally was allowed to visit his pal's district, some half a mile from Peter's own home. More usually, Tommy consorted with the boys who lived around about. They were not of the Catholic faith – indeed, in most cases they seemed not to be of any faith – and they attended one of the two county primary schools in the immediate vicinity.

This mattered not a jot to Tommy, who made up for not being in their company on schooldays by mixing with them as frequently as the weather and parental permission allowed. Thus he cemented friendships with Brian, Alec, Eric, Ronnie, Dave, Stuart and in particular, Robert. He found a particular kindred spirit in Robert.

Robert was a few months older than Tommy. In other ways they were even closer. They each had an older sibling and they shared similar tastes and fears. Robert was the more forceful character but Tommy more than matched him in the brains department. They both had an equal loathing of the opposite sex and of any adult who failed to understand, let alone indulge, two harmless young lads.

One Saturday morning a handful of the boys met as agreed at the corner of Percy Street and Bradshaw Street. From there they set off across the main road and along Causey Foot. They were bound for Delph Mount. Passing the last of the houses, they reached the rough track that led to the disused quarry. This had been used as a council tip for some time and was thus partially filled in. First of all they came to a cluster of garages which had been constructed on the wasteland in a curving line. Tommy's dad rented one of these garages for the family car.

Past the line of garages they came to the edge of the tip, marked by a neat slope where the rubble and hardcore, with household rubbish mixed in, sloped down to the original quarry floor. This was splendid adventure country. There were puddles, hummocks of land, outcrops of bare rock and deep grassy areas.

This was a ready-made wilderness for the boys to act out one of their favourite games resurrected from their visits to the matinees. It was the long knives versus the braves – US cavalry against the ferocious Apaches of Geronimo's tribe.

The Apaches were given a hundred seconds to melt away into the background before the cavalry patrol set out in pursuit.

On this particular occasion, Tommy had chosen to be a savage. He dived into the narrow space between two garages, picking his way carefully over planks, bricks and old paint tins. He thought briefly about hiding behind one of the garages, then dismissed this as being too obvious. Instead, he scrambled up the slope behind the garages and made his way along a ledge that partly skirted the quarry and was about a third of the way to the top.

Tommy found refuge behind a large protruding rock. He was able to peer round this and gain a good view of the quarry floor, which the cavalry patrol would have to cross. Signalling to fellow braves on the opposite side, he settled down with his lance. He had found this splendidly sized stick near one of the allotments they had passed before reaching the garages.

Sure enough, the unsuspecting patrol came into view. Tommy waited while they engaged the braves on the opposite bank in a fierce fire fight.

"*Waah!*" he yelled as he sprang up, loosing off a volley of arrows at the hapless troopers.

As they turned and returned fire, he charged down the slope, whooping and yelling authentically. When he'd got sufficiently close to have proved a point, he then clutched at his chest, having taken a direct hit, and rolled and tumbled downhill until he landed at the soldiers' feet.

The Indians rarely won, as in real life, but they got to play the most dramatic roles as noble losers. Battle was fought several times more, with the boys swapping roles, until tired, hungry and begrimed they called it a day and headed off for home. There would be opportunities to play many more such games this summer, as long as the weather and the light nights held…

That summer lived up to expectations and provided several spells of warm, dry and sunny weather, complete with balmy nights. The local parks were frequented by large numbers of the populace. Families that didn't normally take holidays away from home contented themselves with days spent strolling through the municipal recreational areas. Bowling greens and tennis courts were well used; the former by the older residents and the latter by the more energetic and youthful ones. There were ducks and swans to feed, swings and roundabouts to be played on and regular summer entertainment laid on to amuse the work weary.

The local bands gave concert performances in the open air, using the bandstands provided in both Victoria and Marsden parks. The open air swimming lido in Marsden was saturated with visitors at weekends and on the hotter evenings. As well as the annual funfair and gala, there were the fortnightly home matches of the local cricket club, which competed in the Lancashire League.

The Nelson eleven, like the other league teams, was led by a professional cricketer of international renown. His presence, and that of the opposing pro, was guaranteed to add a thousand or two extra spectators at the matches. These were contested on the splendid ground at Seedhill, alongside the football pitch which had once housed a team competing in the football league.

The cricket team was one of the better in the league and had a long record of success, going back to the halcyon days when a certain ground-breaking West Indian pro was at the helm. The legendary Learie Constantine regularly drew crowds of thousands down to the ground in the 1920s when he plied his magic in front of the most partisan and parochial spectators.

Tommy was more fortunate than many of his peers. The Calverts religiously took a fortnight's holiday every year, courtesy of the hard-working and providential savings of Mum and Dad. Furthermore, they didn't just repair to one of the local resorts like Blackpool or Southport: like Morecambe, such places were fine for day trips but not for the eagerly awaited annual holiday. Mr and Mrs Calvert were a little more ambitious and set their sights further afield. The West Country was the usual attraction because of its almost guaranteed fine weather, by British standards, and the abundance of caravan holiday parks.

The Calverts may not have been able to afford hotels, and probably would have shunned them anyway, but they were able to book a large caravan each year on a park somewhere close to the seaside – an essential prerequisite.

This year Dorset was the chosen location. As well as the two children, Shirley's friend Kathleen had also been invited. That was fine for her, but what about Tommy? Any disappointment that Tommy felt was quickly forgotten when the Automobile Association travel plan that Dad had ordered arrived through the post. He spent many an evening before the big day browsing through the booklet, tracing the route with his finger and mouthing the names of the many towns through which they would pass.

Tommy had been given the honour of helping Dad by acting as navigator. He would be allowed to sit with the route planner on his knee and call out each junction and change of direction. It was a big responsibility, but one that Shirley couldn't do. After all, she was a girl, and anyway she would be too busy nattering with her best friend.

The best part was the night before the holiday. Already the population in the area was falling as quite a few families made an early start to their precious week – or if lucky, fortnight – away. The Calverts spent a frantic and excited evening getting ready for an early morning start on the Saturday.

Dad had brought the car round from the garage. Into the boot was piled the luggage, not just clothing but also food carefully hoarded, and bedding and towelling for the caravan. Mum's task was to prepare the food to be eaten during the long ride. All this meant that darkness was drawing in by the time the car was loaded up and driven back to the garage for the night.

Tommy, and in truth Shirley, were too excited to sleep easily anyway. They would be woken bleary eyed at 5.30 a.m. on the day of departure. By 6.45, they would be heading due south with Tommy reeling off the list of turnings once they were out of familiar territory. By 9.30 a.m. he was fast asleep with his head on Shirley's shoulder while Dad drove effortlessly and purposely onwards.

The first stop, by popular request, was a toilet break in some nameless settlement in Staffordshire. As they all piled out of the car to stretch cramped and weary limbs, Tommy was despatched to the newsagents down the road in order to buy himself a comic and some sweets for everyone to suck en route.

"Hey, come back!" yelled Shirley.

"What do you want?" cried Tommy as he returned.

"Get a comic for Kathleen and me as well," she instructed, pressing a sixpence into his palm. Tommy knew the one she would want; the boring one that was no use to him.

An early lunch was partaken of in a lay-by on the A38 between Worcester and Gloucester. More yawning, arm stretching and leg shaking took place, to the accompaniment of the roar and thunder of goods and holiday traffic hurtling along in both directions.

It would be mid-afternoon before the travel weary party finally drew in to the holiday caravan park near Bridport and pulled up by the "Arrivals" sign.

The Holiday

F aces pressed against the car windows as the Calvert family took in the panorama of the leisure park. Dad had gone to the office in the reception block to pay the balance and pick up the caravan keys. There was a small shop with a sort of café area, a separate concrete structure with various doors and small windows. They knew from experience that this would contain things like a laundry room and possibly shower and toilet block.

The park, like many of its type at the time, was not endowed with much by way of on-site amusement and leisure provision. This suited the family. They didn't want to be sharing the site with the sort of families who would usually take their break in a holiday camp complete with uniforms, swimming pools, playparks and restaurants. After all, they had a car and they wished to go forth exploring the delights of the West Country, not spend their time on site.

Dad emerged brandishing his bunch of keys and pointed towards the next field as he clambered back into the driving seat. They set off, passing several occupied caravans – at least they had vehicles parked alongside. Passing through a gate, they entered a second field. The whole scene very much resembled a farm for livestock, which it probably had been before its transformation.

Dad drove on past three, four and more vans on both sides of the track. Eventually, just as he began to turn a corner, they spotted the likely suspect. The number on the side matched the one on the key ring. It was not the most modern van on the park. Liveried in cream and pale brown with net curtains, it looked rather unprepossessing, at least to Shirley and Mum, and no doubt Shirley's friend Kathleen.

Undaunted, Dad climbed from the car with Tommy in close attendance. Pushing the key into the lock, he opened the door and stepped inside. At least it smelt clean. Tommy followed and ran into the far end. He clambered onto the bench seating, pulled aside the curtains and waved to Mum and the girls just as they emerged from the car.

Having overcome their initial reservations, the group set about unpacking the luggage and rearranging it inside the caravan. A kettle was set to boil as soon as Mr Calvert had sorted out the gas supply.

"Where are we sleeping?" whined Shirley, speaking on behalf of her friend.

"In the two bunks at the far end," explained Dad.

This led Tommy to the conclusion that he must be destined to occupy the narrow bed in the centre of the caravan that would be made up once the bench seat had been rearranged. Mum and Dad, of course, would have the dining area which would become a double bed with some deft cushion switching.

And so the Calverts settled in to enjoy a fortnight of rest and, hopefully, fun and enjoyment.

Shirley had her friend for company. Tommy, not being short of imagination, found plenty to fascinate him in the surrounding fields and especially along the shore. He particularly loved scrambling over the rocks above the beach, exploring the hollows in the cliff side and the pools left by the receding tide.

There was the small on-site amusement arcade for closer at hand play times. It was there that Tommy met Andy, a lad of the same age who had come down from London for his holiday a week earlier.

"Wot's yor name then?" asked the new boy in a dialect that was quite strange to Tommy.

"Tommy," he replied, as politely as he knew how.

"I'm Andy. I come from Brentford." Seeing the blank look on Tommy's face, he continued, "That's in Sarf London. Wot abaht you?"

"I'm from Lankyshire. A town called Nelson," answered Tommy in a tongue as alien to Andy as his own had proved to Tommy.

Introductions duly complete, the two of them hit it off and spent a few happy mornings and evenings playing together. The afternoons were scheduled by Mr Calvert for trips to surrounding places of interest. Tommy would have preferred to remain on camp with Andy but that wasn't an option.

Breakfast was a highlight of the early morning starts – early because Dad was anxious for them not to waste any time in the precious days. There would be cereals and tinned fruit juice, followed by some sort of fry-up conjured up by mum on the twin gas rings. Then it was a hasty clear away and wash up before donning summer gear for the wonderful day ahead. Only once did they have to don sweaters and tote anoraks for the driving rain. Nothing was going to restrict them to camp for the day.

The girls were recruited to help put up the packed lunch on the days when they decided to make an early start on their explorations.

On some mornings, a more leisurely approach was adopted. On those occasions, while Mr and Mrs Calvert tidied up and rested for a while, the children set out to explore the campsite. Shirley and Kathleen preferred to stroll around seeking sympathetic company or just promenading. Tommy wasn't as boring. When Andy could be found, the two of them went walkabout, mostly through the small wood and down to the shore.

Alas, Andy's family returned home after the first week, leaving Tommy companionless for the second part of the holiday.

The most memorable day out was to Lyme Regis. At least, it was made memorable in the family history for the day when Tommy embarrassed himself.

After a splendid afternoon in the seaside resort, Dad stopped off at a quaint countryside pub on the journey home. The family found a table and seating in the beer garden at the rear and Mr Calvert set off to get the drinks.

"Can I have a cider, please?" cried Tommy to his dad's retreating back.

"Don't be silly, you're too young," mocked Shirley.

"No I'm not. Anyway, cider isn't real drink."

"Course it is," replied Shirley, "isn't it, Kathleen?" Kathleen, being far too polite to take sides in a family dispute, merely smiled and gave a sort of nod which Shirley took as ample confirmation.

Dad duly returned with his pint, a glass of orange juice for mum, two colas for the girls and a half pint of a cloudy amber liquid.

"What's that?" asked Shirley, pointing.

"Well, he asked for cider. They didn't have any bottled stuff so this is some draught scrumpy."

"He can't have that," cried a horrified Mum.

"It'll do him no harm, just the one glass," was Dad's view. "Anyway, I've paid for it now. He asked for it so he can sample it."

A beaming Tommy took a tentative sip and then a large swig. It wasn't sweet like the Bulmer's cider he'd had at home but it quenched his thirst. Shirley took the glass, tasted a mouthful and pulled a face. After half of the drink, Mum wisely took the rest and passed Tommy her orange instead.

It was only when they returned to the car that the effect became apparent. As Tommy went to step up into the rear seat, he missed his footing and went sprawling, his feet sliding back onto the pavement and his top half slumped across the floor in the back of the car. Shirley's face was a mixture of disgust and embarrassment as she hauled him upright and propelled him into the car. She refused to speak to him after that, but the family was spared his further company as he went straight to bed when they returned to the caravan. Actually, he lay on the bench seat at the opposite end from the rest of them. The beds would not be made up until late evening.

They would pass the evening reading, playing cards and listening to the portable radio by the light of the gas mantles. Bedtime was a confusion of storing away the folding table, rearranging the seating cushions, wrestling with sheets and blankets and then undressing in semi-privacy before crawling into the beds. The girls were allowed to sit up reading by gaslight for a while before settling down for the night. Inevitably, Mrs Calvert would have to don dressing gown and slippers for one last trip to the toilet block halfway across the field. This necessitated the carrying of a torch held towards the ground. The purpose of this was to avoid molehills and hollows as well as not to disturb fellow campers.

One particular morning when he was left to his own devices, Tommy went to his favourite part of the rocky shore. He scrambled over boulders, trod through soft shingle, peered into tidal pools and scribbled patterns in to the wet sand. When he judged that it was time to return to base, he leapt back onto the rocks leading to the return path through the trees. He jumped confidently from one outcrop to another. Unfortunately, one of his strides left him landing on the downside of a large rock which was covered in a fine, clinging film of still damp weed.

The one foot which had gained a purchase on this treacherous surface soon parted company with it, leaving Tommy flailing the air in a comical backflip. It could have resulted in a nasty accident. However, the guilty rock ended in a deep pool. Tommy was launched unceremoniously into this, back first. With a splendid splash, he was dumped with arms flailing uselessly into the abyss.

There was enough depth of water to cushion his landing on the bottom. He had managed to close his mouth instinctively after a sharp gasp of surprise, but had a clear view of the swirling water and weeds as he struggled to the surface. He was not a swimmer by any means, nor did he have to be on this occasion.

He struggled to his feet looking a most sorry sight. There were wisps of weed and even some grit and shell tangled in his hair. His tee shirt clung wetly to him while his shorts sagged pitifully between his legs. He blew in and out several times, feeling very sorry for himself as he dripped over the rocks. Shaking his arms and legs, he set off for home. Every step resulted in a squelchy squeak from his sandals as he left a soaking spoor along the path.

Shirley and Kathleen were just coming around from the reception block when they both pointed in his direction and let out a shriek and a peal of laughter.

That was enough to set Tommy off. "Shurrup you!" he wailed pitifully as he dripped towards them.

"Look at the state of you," replied Shirley, rather unnecessarily and unkindly. "What's mum going to say?"

Tommy disdained to reply as he plodded homeward.

He wasn't allowed inside the caravan in that state, of course, and had to suffer the indignity of being disrobed outdoors by Dad while a smirking big sister held a bath towel discreetly around him.

All too soon, such enriching experiences and enjoyable episodes came to a conclusion. The fortnight had passed exceedingly quickly and sunny days in the embrace of Dorsetshire would give way to the harsher surrounds of East Lancashire. The holiday would be stored in the memory and would sustain Mr and Mrs Calvert through the autumn as they toiled to provide and to save for their next escape. As soon as Christmas had passed, they would begin to plan for this.

Tommy and Robert in their Local Area

T he skin on the warm tar wrinkled as his forefinger continued to push it aside. It reminded Tommy of the waves he had seen from the cliff top overlooking Lulworth Cove, which the family had visited on their holiday the previous summer. His finger and thumb reached into the crevice between the cobblestones where his marble had lodged. Tommy delicately held the rescued marble close to his face where he could detect not only the wonderfully swirled blue and green heart but the tiny scratches and wear marks on the surface.

"I'll play you again but I've only got three more ollies left," shrilled a rather disgruntled Robert.

Tommy nodded his assent and fired off the rescued marble across the flagstones from where it bounced against the stone garden wall of Number 17 and came to rest on a grass-filled groove between two stones. Robert's first shot scored a glancing hit on the overworked target, causing it to rear up and lose another tiny shard of its fading surface when crash landing on the unforgiving cobbles.

"You jammy beggar!" yelled Tommy as he retrieved both marbles and handed them over to the victorious Robert. "Right. That's it. I'm going in now for me tea."

Leaving Robert to exult at his final winning play, Tommy pistoned his legs into a sudden burst of speed that enabled him to dummy the lamppost as well as the Spurs full-back before crashing the phantom ball in off the Tottenham crossbar. He slowed down to acknowledge the cheers of the crowd and the back slapping of his jubilant team-mates before unlatching the backyard gate to return to the dressing room. The morning papers would carry the astounding headline of the youngest goal scorer in the First Division – nine-year-old Tommy Calvert, surely destined to play for England.

"Is that you, Tommy? About time you came in – now get your hands washed. I'm putting your tea out," shrilled a weary voice from the steam filled kitchen.

"OK Mum. What's for tea?" Tommy called back as he raced upstairs to carry out his mother's order. He only heard the "liver and—" bit of Mum's reply as he turned into the small bathroom. He looked with distaste at his sister's underwear and stockings draped over the folding clothes rack balanced in the bath. Leaning forward, he peered at his image in the small shelf mirror and chuckled as he was greeted with a raspberry by a flushed, round-faced and pop-eyed alter ego made even more elfin by a hank of dark brown hair flapping across his brow. After a fleeting encounter between his grubby hands and the half melted bar of Palmolive, followed by a splurge of cold water, Tommy emerged to skip down the stairs two at a time, with the help of the banister rail, before diving into his usual chair.

Dad looked up from his newspaper. "How come you're always last to come in and first to sit down for your dinner?" he remarked, not expecting a sensible reply. He wasn't disappointed as Tommy merely shrugged his shoulders at the same time as putting out his tongue at Shirley. She tried to ignore the taunt as a thirteen-year-old should when goaded by a young twerp, but instead found herself forming what she hoped was a withering look of disgust. Tommy wasn't impressed. He wriggled impatiently on his chair until the others joined him at the table, each one receiving a steaming plate of mashed potato, liver and onions.

Less than five minutes later, Tommy's knife and fork clattered onto a food-free plate. Only a smear of gravy betrayed the fact that a large helping of dinner had once rested there.

"Are you off out *again*?" said Dad to Tommy's retreating back. His only answer was the rattle of the latch on the backyard gate as it swung to a close in response to Tommy's hefty tug. "Ask a silly question!" he muttered, more to himself than to any sympathetic ear.

When he reached the end of the street where the marbles battle had been conducted, Tommy found it deserted save for the scrawny tabby which lived at Number 28 and which was lazily licking at its paw before drawing it behind and around its ear in a flannelling action. Now, where had Robert gone? How selfish of him not to have gone for his tea at the same time as Tommy had done. Now he'd have to find something else to do – he couldn't go back home so soon.

Tommy decided to wander down to the main road and across to the long row of bungalows on the opposite side. He would explore the spare land by the allotments. Walking along the pavement past the bungalows, Tommy liked to run his hands gently through those funny plants, bursting with little purple or white blossom, which overhung the walls and kept on growing down towards the pavement like a giant's beard. They were his favourites because they were different and his own tiny front garden had none.

As he had half expected, there was no one else on the field. Shrugging off his disappointment, Tommy ran over to the deep ditch which coursed diagonally across the area. He leapt for the opposite side. Almost but not quite reaching the top, his spreadeagled form slid backwards down the slippery grassy bank until his feet abruptly met the floor of the ditch. Unperturbed as well as completely unconcerned about the slick of greasy brown mud on both kneecaps, he grabbed fistfuls of grass tufts and hauled himself up the opposite bank. He paused near the top.

Craning his neck, he peered into the no man's land in front of him. It wouldn't do to have his head blown off by an alert German machine-gunner on the lookout for an intrepid but careless Tommy like himself. The coast was clear so he scampered across to the outpost, remembering to keep his head low.

As he paused for breath with both hands grabbing on to the rotting wooden fence, Tommy spotted the stooping figure of Old Harry working on his allotment. Harry paused in his digging, looked up, and recognising the young figure called out, "Oh, it's you. All right, lad?"

He called everyone lad, even though he well knew Tommy's name.

Tommy shouted back, "Hiya Harry! Wot yer doing?"

Harry groaned with relief as his stiffly arched back shrugged off the ache caused by his stooping labour. When he felt sufficiently recovered he replied, "Just hoeing round my veggies and suchlike. You can come over and have a stick o' me rhubarb if you like. There's loads of it this year."

Tommy stepped over a gap in the broken fence. Taking care to tread carefully between the plants on the neighbouring plot, he walked round the path leading to Harry's section, lifted and swung the gate (it had long since failed to move on its hinges, which were in any case hanging off) until he could pass through and then he carefully manhandled the gate back into position. He stood waiting.

Old Harry wiped his sweat soaked palms on the legs of his baggy pants before reaching down to snap off a thick stalk of pink and green rhubarb and offer it across. Tommy snapped off the large, insect nibbled, lacy leaf from the top, which took with it a section of rhubarb stalk from the side as he pulled it clear. Thrusting the other end into his mouth, Tommy took an enthusiastic bite and almost at once screwed up his cheeks as the acidly sweet fibres succumbed to his crunching teeth. He felt his jaw muscles tightening at the tart sensation but still carried on with a second plucky bite. It was nice really, but it would have tasted better sprinkled with sugar and baked in a pie by his mum.

Finding a mound of fairly solid heaped soil and dried grass sods on which to sit, Tommy settled down to work on his treat while watching Harry labouring away. He became briefly fascinated by a dewdrop hanging from Harry's nostril which kept wobbling but which steadfastly refused to detach itself despite Harry's energetics. When the old man finally stood up and ended the spectacle by pulling out a crumpled, soiled hankie and snorting into it, Tommy took that as a signal to lever himself up from the mound, brush off some of the damp vegetation clinging to the seat of his pants, and wander off, calling back a cheerio and a thanks to Harry.

Halfway along the row of bungalows Tommy began to pump his legs until he was in a near flat-out sprint that took him across the main road and along Bentley Street. He slowed to a head-pounding walk as his calf muscles protested at the unwarranted strain. Still no Robert! Even the lazy tabby had departed for newer territory.

Well, I'm not going home yet, decided a defiant but crestfallen Tommy, as if he needed to convince himself that such a move would be unwise. Instead, he retraced his steps to the main road, crossed over to the waste ground by the railway line and hoisted himself up onto the top of the wooden fence that served as a boundary marking off the forbidden swathe of land belonging to British Railways that bordered the twin tracks. He peered both up and down the line. Nothing – no passenger train; not a sign of anything mechanical and mobile.

Tommy let out a resigned sigh. He picked up a loose stone and hurled it at the trackside warning notice. He was rewarded by a satisfying metallic clang as the stone ricocheted off and dropped to rest by the sleepers. It was at that moment that he happened to see two girls walking along the road that ran parallel to the railway line but on the other side of the tracks. Wasn't one of them Wendy Foster – she of the snobby family who lived near the top of Bradshaw Street and who attended the county primary school of the same name farther down? Tommy yelled out something indecipherable, and when the girls turned to investigate the noise, made a rude grimace and gesture and promptly hared off back towards familiar territory.

At about the same time, a stocky young lad with a shock of spiky blond hair pulled shut the door of Atkins' corner shop clutching a tightly screwed paper bag containing 3d worth of liquorice torpedoes. He hadn't taken more than half a dozen carefully placed toe steps across the street cobbles, being particular not to trespass on a gap, when he heard the familiar cry,

"Hey, Robert Bobert, wot yer doin'?"

Recognising the source of the cry even before he looked up, Robert hastily crammed his bag of goodies into the pocket of his crumpled khaki shorts. This ploy had not gone unnoticed by Tommy, who sprinted up to meet him, delighted to have found a kindred spirit – even one who tried to hide his sweets from his best pal. Rummaging in his other pocket in an effort to distract his friend, Robert's hand eventually emerged with a worn penny. Holding it aloft, he gestured towards the chewing gum dispensing machine bolted to the shop wall.

"I've got a penny here! Let's see if we're lucky on that." He nodded at the contraption.

All the local children were well versed in the workings of this fiendish machine, which held the promise of a double payout every fourth turn. Tommy was first to peer at the knob on the side and he let out a groan as the arrow was pointing to the sky. Everyone knew that it had to be at the nine o'clock position for the promise of treasure.

"What hard luck!" gasped Tommy. "It's only one more

move away. That's the closest I've seen it for weeks!"

"Well, I'm not putting my penny in just so some other jammy sod can get the double packet next time," protested Robert.

"Tell you what – I'll go home and get one of my pennies and then we'll split the winnings," enthused Tommy. Taking a shrug of the shoulders for assent, Tommy hared off to fetch the vital cash. Robert stood guard. He adopted what he considered to be an air of nonchalance. He leant idly against the wall, careful to conceal the giveaway knob and determined to repel any intruder who might beat them to the prize. Soon enough, Tommy returned brandishing his coin and calling to Robert to set the plan in motion by putting in his penny. This Robert did by carefully sliding in the head of King George V until the coin dropped with a satisfying clunk. He turned the knob anti-clockwise until it pointed to nine o'clock. He was immediately rewarded with the sight and sound of a single four-pack of the pillow shaped gum tumbling into the bottom tray. Tommy then gleefully stepped forward and put his rather shinier penny into the slot. With tongue stuck out and concentrating like a safe breaker, Tommy dialled the quarter turn and held his hand over the tray to catch the *single packet* of gum!

"Hey, look at that! It's supposed to give us two."

Both boys looked incredulously at the knob on the side of the machine. Sure enough, it was now facing six o'clock and that meant that two packets should have dropped out. Robert pummelled on the machine with a clenched fist, which only resulted in the tall, angular figure of Mr Atkins emerging to see who was vandalising his property.

"What's going on here?" he enquired rather unnecessarily, as he could see that the two cheeky beggars were trying to get free chewing gum by abusing the mechanism. "Clear off before I tell your parents," he threatened, oblivious to any effect that such a threat might have on future custom from the two boys.

"But we won two packs of gum fair and square and the machine didn't—"

That was as far as Tommy got before Mr Atkins' raised hand rendered any further discussion redundant. The two boys scarpered before his hand could connect, and hopefully before he decided to tell their parents anyway.

When they reached the safety of back Ponden Street two blocks away, the boys huddled together to confer.

"That wasn't fair," protested Robert.

"Why d'yer think it didn't give out two packs of gum?" pondered Tommy.

"Maybe the machine has run out and old skinflint Atkins hasn't refilled it."

Tommy nodded vigorously in agreement before vowing, "Next time I go in that shop I'm nicking something to make up for that. It's only fair, innit?"

Robert agreed, at the same time thinking that he wouldn't like to be the one trying to outwit old Mr Atkins.

"Old" Mr Atkins, who was all of thirty-seven years of age, had by then retreated indoors with a shake of his head, surprised at the devastating effect he had had on the two boys and knowing that he wouldn't have dared to actually hit them. "Ah well, it does no harm to let them think I'll stand no nonsense," he mused.

When the coast was clear, the boys walked around to the front of the street and perched on the short stone wall fronting the tiny garden of Number 5. Wriggling about for comfort, they sat upon their hands until they were each able to settle on a patch of cold coping stone that didn't touch any exposed thigh. That was the trouble with short trousers.

"Anyway, what about those sweets in your pocket – give us one," demanded Tommy.

Robert gave a sigh of resignation, knowing he couldn't refuse his best mate, and duly handed over two torpedoes, making sure that one of them was a pink one. Having dispensed such generosity, Robert took advantage by declaring with exaggerated indignation, "By the way, my name's Robert Berry not Robert Bobert for your information!"

The admonition was dismissed with a shrug of the shoulders from Tommy. As if the exchange had not taken place, both boys set about gleefully sucking the end of a pink torpedo each and proceeded to rub the sticky wet end across their lips in a grotesque parody of older sisters applying lipstick. Unabashed, they made pouting mouths at each other before licking off the evidence with greedy tongues. They didn't see anything peculiar in this little act. Didn't everyone do that with torpedoes? They then repeated the move with blue torpedoes, making their grins even more hideous.

"Oh, yeah," remembered Tommy, "I saw Wendy wotsit with that other stuck-up twit Annie when I was down near the railway."

"What did yer do?" asked Robert, adding, "Did they look like this?" as he sucked in his lips and fluttered his eyelashes in a passing imitation of a girl trying to elicit a kiss from some unfortunate young lad.

Tommy howled with glee, both at the parody and at the ridiculous expression on his friend's face. "You look like that Violet Elizabeth wotsit in the William books," he chortled. "Wotsit" was the boys' favourite word for anybody or anything that they couldn't remember and also looked on with not a little disdain.

Having cheered up considerably since their run-in with Mr Atkins, the two best mates slid off the garden wall. Grinning happily, they strolled round the corner. The smiles froze on their faces when they saw, coming towards them, the two adult sisters whose names were unknown to all the local children. It was the sight of the figure between them that was the real cause of contrition with the boys. For holding hands with one of the ladies and stumbling along between them was the poor blind boy who everyone knew by sight but not name.

He walked with a peculiar jerking action as if he couldn't control his muscles properly. He was about the same age as Robert and Tommy, which only made the sight more poignant, at least to the two of them. They both made embarrassed, sheepish grins before looking away so that no one could accuse them of staring at the pitiful sight. The sisters were quite used to such responses and acted as if the pair were not even present. When they had passed and reached a sufficiently safe distance, Robert stage whispered to Tommy, "Everyone says he was born blind, don't they?"

"Yeah, that must be horrible. Fancy never ever knowing what anything looks like. I wonder what he thinks things around him look like, poor sod," pondered Tommy.

"Well, I'm glad I'm not blind and I hope I never am," stated Robert with great conviction.

Thus considerably chastened, the two moved on along Percy Street until they reached the corner where Miss Boocock's grocery shop replaced the terraced house that would normally have completed the block. They stepped up onto the forecourt, which substituted for a front garden, and peered in through the large window. The advertising poster stuck to the window never failed to attract some attention, proclaiming as it did that a penny-farthing could purchase an Oxo cube. The message was imaginatively enhanced by a drawing of the strange cycle with a penny for the front wheel and a farthing for the rear. Completing the image was a grinning cyclist holding aloft a jug of the magic brew.

The shop was closed now but the boys continued to eye the displays, scanning past cans, packets and tins for a sight of something interesting. Apart from a dead wasp lying next to a bottle of Camp Coffee – another product with an eye-catching label depicting a cheery Scottish soldier complete with kilt – there was nothing more to tempt them or even to hold their attention any longer.

After considerately peeling off a few slivers of hard brown paint from the windowsill, thus exposing even more of Miss Boocock's shop front woodwork to the ravages of the weather, they walked on for another half block before tacitly admitting defeat, assisted by the looming deep grey clouds that had seemingly suddenly materialised overhead. They muttered farewells and each turned in their respective directions for home and dragged themselves away.

Going Down Town

It was quite a bright Saturday morning for mid-October and the fresh breeze had already begun to dry off the pavement slabs, which still glistened from the overnight rain. Tommy was on his way to the town centre, not with any particular purpose in mind but merely to pass the time. He loved to stroll at random, stopping at will and wherever the mood took him. On this occasion his ramble took him to the model shop close to the railway arch that spanned the street of the same name and which led to the main shopping area.

Pressing his face to the window, Tommy gazed admiringly at the array of the finest locomotives that Hornby Dublo had created for the delight of those fortunate children possessed of sufficient funds or generous relatives who could afford them. He particularly liked the tiny sculptured figures and buildings that were made in order to transform a toy train set into an authentic representation of an English landscape. In his mind's eye he pictured the layout that he would own if he were rich. There would be tunnels for the trains, green fields full of livestock, quaint villages and a little station with two platforms and a signal box.

With a sigh of bliss mingled with longing, he leaned away from the glass, leaving behind a foggy patch and a greasy spot marking where his nose and face had made contact with it. He turned to see the display in the window on the other side of the door. Tommy gazed enthusiastically for a while at the plastic kits offering models of Spitfires, Messerschmitts, destroyers, submarines and other powerful symbols of the war.

He admired the evocative pictures on the boxes, which depicted the magnificent machines in stirring action, but had little longing to possess the contents – consisting as they did of flat, lifeless grey plastic parts with tubes of glue and cigarette papers giving instructions for recreating them. At least the shiny metal steam engines were complete and ready for immediate use.

Tommy turned away from the display and instantly found his face filled with a smothering blanket of heavy blue wool. On recovering from the shock, he grinned sheepishly and muttered his apologies to the wool, realising that he had walked headlong into the stomach of a large and rather severe looking woman, who responded with something which sounded to Tommy like, "Harrumph... tsk, little creature!" He continued down the street with head bowed to avoid further embarrassment from any onlookers.

When he reached the centre of town and the pavement by the traffic lights at the main junction, he swivelled his head right to left and up. Judging the moment to be safe enough, he sprinted across the road and reached sanctuary by the Lord Nelson Hotel without mishap. He then walked down Market Street and past the Grand Cinema until he arrived at the Market Hall. This was another favourite venue for Tommy, who could spend many a happy hour patrolling the aisles between the stalls and drinking in the sights, sounds and mingled aromas.

He was scanning the stalls lining the centre aisle for the second time when he spotted Mad Jimmy shuffling towards him. Everyone knew Mad Jimmy, and the children especially regarded him with a mixture of awe and apprehension. He was a jolly character but, it was rumoured, was just as likely to lash out at you as to ignore you or – even worse – fix you with a smile. Tommy pretended to look at the haberdashery on the nearest stall but kept a clear bead on Jimmy.

"Nah then, Jimmy!" cried the white-overalled figure on the pet stall, causing Tommy to jump. "What yer down for this morning?"

Jimmy grinned toothily and then sparred with the air before him as if to belabour the caller before muttering, "Awreet, 'n 'ow are you, you mad bugger?"

At least that's what his reply sounded like to Tommy. Finally noticing the lad, Jimmy made a feint towards him, still with raised fists. Tommy's heart skipped a beat and he only recovered when Jimmy laughed hugely before moving on. The pet stall holder noticed Tommy's confusion and sought to reassure him. "He's harmless enough is Jimmy."

Tommy wasn't so sure. He walked rather more swiftly to the top doors and emerged on to the street, casting his eyes both ways quickly to make sure that Jimmy wasn't still around. He strode off, more boldly than he felt. Crossing the street by the chip shop, he paused to give his senses a treat.

The chippy door was open. Swathed in steam, the large sweaty woman in white cap and pinafore was vigorously tapping the basket full of chips on the fryer rim to shake off the excess fat. Even from the pavement Jimmy could imbibe the rich vapours, especially the pungent vinegary one that seemed to penetrate his eyes as well as his ears. She beckoned him in.

Not wanting to refuse such a direct request from an adult, but conscious of the fact that his pockets were empty, Jimmy cautiously stepped inside. He was soon reassured. With finger on lips to ensure his silence, and a quick glance at the rear of the shop, Mrs Chippy doled out a handful of chips onto a sheet of newspaper, deftly applied salt and vinegar with one huge hand and thrust the prize towards Tommy, shooing him out of the shop. Tommy didn't need a second invitation. Cottoning on to her conspiracy, he hastily withdrew.

When he had reached a safe distance from the chippy – he half expected to be pursued by the irate owner – Tommy opened the screwed-up parcel. Grinning, he popped a large chip into his mouth and instantly wished that he hadn't. His mouth opened wide to expel the mad hot sensation. Fanning himself with a wildly flapping hand, he gasped and blew in an effort to lessen the searing pain. The vinegar stung the back of his nose, almost making him sneeze. That was enough. His hand closed round the paper to seal in the contents. He would wait a while before risking another mouthful.

Crossing the main road once again, Tommy entered the small covered arcade with its handful of shops. In truth it was a modest section of the town's retail centre, but to Tommy it held a particular fascination. There was the sports shop owned by a former player for Preston North End. This contained, as well as a wealth of expensive sports equipment, various memorabilia associated with its owner's sporting past. This collection included a photograph of the Wembley Cup Final line-up of 1938 depicting the teams, including yours truly, being presented to the Duke of Kent. Tommy always spent some time gazing at this particular photo, mentally drifting off until he could picture himself as the captain of the Preston team proudly introducing his lads to the Duke before the kick-off. Not that Tommy was a North End fan, you understand, but just to be there at Wembley – wow!

Tommy had a great love for the noble game, nurtured by his dad's indulgence in taking him along every Saturday afternoon to his local works team's fixture in the Amateur League. He had even bought Tommy a pair of the high, lace-up brown boots with solid toecaps used by all the adult players. Never mind that they weighed heavy on Tommy's feet or that every time he tried to kick the cannonball that passed for a football in his dad's works team he got a severe shock that transmitted up his leg and sent his heel cannon-ing into the heel of his boot and resulted in painful blistering. When he grew up, he was going to follow in the footsteps of "Tiny" Clinton or "Jaffa" Jeffreys who regularly performed heroics for the factory eleven.

"Gosh! Is that the time?" queried a shocked Tommy to no one in particular as he looked up at the ornate dial on the large clock face on the tower above Barclay's Bank. It registered 12.10 p.m. and Tommy panicked as he imagined his dad getting ready to leave for the afternoon's football. Surely he won't go without me, he thought, but then answered his own surmise with a gloomy realisation that he would indeed – in fact if his dad didn't get to the rendez-vous point by 1.00 p.m. the match would be in jeopardy.

Tommy set off at a hectic sprint towards home. How he ran! Up Railway Street, through the pedestrian underpass which ducked beneath the railway track to Burnley and beyond, and then labouring up the long uphill stretch of Hibson Road which led to the streets of his neighbourhood. By now he was gasping for breath, despite his assertion that he was a healthy specimen. To be fair he had run flat-out most of the way, until the incline took its toll.

Pausing momentarily to give respite to his heaving lungs and wobbly legs, Tommy leaned drunkenly on the stone wall by the bottom of the steps leading to his house. He somehow managed to climb these and push open the front and vestibule doors. Barely acknowledging Tiggy, the family tabby of whom Tommy was really rather fond, he strolled into the living room as casually as his physical state allowed.

"Mam, where's Dad?" he pleaded as he realised that Dad was not around.

"He's out the back just checking out the car," replied Mam, not at all appreciative of the need for urgency in her son's enquiry. "He's nearly ready to go so if you're going with him you'd better shift yourself."

Tommy immediately darted out through the kitchen door to check that Dad was indeed still around and hadn't set off without him. The very idea!

"C'mon, son, you'd better get a move on if you're coming," said Dad rather superfluously.

"I'll just get my boots first," replied Tommy as he ducked back inside. Moments later he emerged clutching the well dubbined brown boots with leather studs that were authentic copies of the footgear worn by all the professional players. They were his pride and joy and had been ever since last Christmas when he had first cast eyes on his wonderful present. Ever since, they had not gone short of a liberal application of dubbin each week, usually administered on Sundays after the mud of the day before had been scraped off with an old bone-handled knife. This ritual was usually performed by Tommy in the backyard, weather permitting, on a bed of old newspapers.

Tommy reached for the chrome door handle of the Austin Ten saloon and swung open the rear door. Once he was safely settled in the back (this was his ordained place as Dad had to pick up two or three of the works team en route to the game), he ventured to ask, "Who are we playing today?"

By now Dad had set off and reached the end of the back street where the car was always parked when brought from the garage. He looked both ways although there was no other traffic around; in fact only a handful of cars regularly plied the streets around home. Having satisfied himself that he could continue to the main road, Dad attended to Tommy's enquiry. "It's North Valley Rangers away today, son."

Tommy was familiar with the name and also the venue. They were the runners-up the previous season – a useful outfit with some uncompromising and forbidding looking defenders. Their home turf was an undulating meadow festooned with the droppings of the flock of sheep that occasionally shared the pitch with the players, though thankfully not on match days. Conditions would not favour the skilful football usually employed by Jaffa and co.

Having stopped at the prearranged rendezvous by Timothy White's chemists to pick up Phil and Archie, Dad proceeded to the ground after enquiring, "Where's Jackie then?"

Jackie being Archie's younger brother who played inside forward, the latter felt obliged to inform Tommy's dad, "Oh, he's been round to see his girlfriend this morning and he's making his own way from there."

The approach to the "pitch" took them along a bumpy farm lane (home of the aforementioned sheep) and onto a patch of bare ground by a barn. Seemingly undeterred by the agricultural surroundings, the players, closely followed by a frantically pacing Tommy anxious to keep up, strode purposefully up to the archway into the barn. Pushing open the manure-encrusted wooden door, they entered the gloomy interior. Tommy's nostrils were immediately assailed by an extremely pungent and ammonia laden atmosphere that assaulted the eyes as well as the nose.

Checking the wooden bench for any offensive deposits, Tommy jumped up and squirmed into a reasonably comfortable perch, swinging his legs, which failed to reach the floor by a good six inches. The players who had arrived with Tommy and his dad immediately set about their pre-match preparations. Tommy was well versed in this ritual, having attended most of the season's games. Out from their holdalls came boots, thick cane-strengthened shin pads, trunks (or alternatively, jockstraps), assorted bandages and strips of material and various medicine bottles.

By now the barn changing room was beginning to fill with the appearance and sounds of the other team members arriving to much jocularity and leg pulling. Tommy drank all this in and watched fascinated as this collection of factory hands slowly transformed themselves into gladiators girding themselves for the forthcoming confrontation.

Eventually, after much adult factory talk that largely passed Tommy by, the players were almost ready. The final touch was needed. Off came the medicine bottle lids, out splurged a generous helping of thick fluid into palms, followed by the vigorous application of this fluid onto thighs and calfs accompanied by much slapping. All Tommy knew was that this powerful potion was designed to lubricate muscles and, in severe weather, offer protection from the cold. He had heard names such as wintergreen and horse liniment used to describe these fluids. Whatever, they smelt suspiciously like the barn when they first entered it!

The Local Football Match

M r Calvert had organised his emergency kit, consisting of bucket of cold water complete with sponge, basic first aid sundries and spare football. Tommy was allowed to carry this proudly out to the arena. With a loud clattering of studs on flagged floor, the team walked out into the pale autumn sunlight and broke into a trot to reach the far side of the pitch. Tommy was fascinated by the plumes of steam emanating from the heads of the Victory Works team players' mouths and nostrils. Though he knew that this was due to the sharp autumnal air, he couldn't help imagining that his heroes were breathing dragon fire in anticipation of the forthcoming clash with their enemies.

The home team had already commandeered the nearest goalmouth, which also happened to be the least undulating and contained fewer sheep droppings. Tommy strode round the perimeter of the pitch clutching the spare ball. When he reached the far end, he lifted the ball above his head and hurled it onto the pitch with both hands, just like a throw-in. It was trapped on the thigh by Bobby Lambert, the strapping wing-half, who then swung a boot and volleyed it towards his own keeper.

Mr Calvert then called Tommy over to assist him with the pitch marking. It seemed that the home team were lacking in support and so the two of them were required to do their bit. Tommy thrust his hands into the large sack and emerged clutching a handful of coarse sawdust. This action caused a miniature dust cloud to puff up into his face. When he had blinked several times to clear some of the finer sawdust from his eyes and spat out some more that he had inhaled, he set about the task of line marking. This involved walking backwards in as straight a line as possible and shaking his hands to release some of the dust to mark the touchline.

It took him several trips to the sack to make a line from the metal goalpost to the corner flag (not that there was a flag there). The only indication that he had reached the full half-width of the pitch was the fact that he was only six feet from the dilapidated stone wall of the pasture. He then set about covering the stretch from the corner to the halfway line. The end result was a trail of sawdust some four inches wide which weaved its way drunkenly from side to side as well as up and down the ridges and hollows of the rough turf. No one, least of all the referee, ever seemed to criticise the end result. Probably they were just grateful that someone had at least made the effort.

The match got underway. There was much running, enthusiastic hoofing of the ball and shouting for a while without either goal being under much threat. When the home team did manage to open the scoring, Tommy's interest waned and he busied himself trundling the spare ball across the field behind the goal. He did manage to kick it hard enough that it rolled onto the pitch just as the opposing team were mounting an attack. This confused the North Valley winger who was momentarily faced with a choice of two balls to centre. He ended up selecting the correct one but made such a hash of the cross that the Victory keeper was able to gather the ball safely.

Tommy scampered onto the pitch to retrieve his errant ball and was met with a glare by the unfortunate winger. The lumbering presence of the Victory wing-half, Bobby, prevented further discourse on the matter. Bobby kicked Tommy's ball away with a conspiratorial grin aimed at the lad. Surely, thought Tommy, he didn't think I did it deliberately to help out! The very thought sent him sheepishly edging away from the defensive area before either the ref or his dad could berate him.

Surely enough, as Tommy knew they would, the lads managed an equaliser. The fact that at the vital moment in the action his attention was distracted by the bellowing of an over-laden cow in the adjacent field did not diminish in any way the enormity of the occasion. The goal must surely have come about via a thunderbolt from the right boot of Jaffa. Strange how the North Valley defenders were arguing among themselves and gesticulating at their crestfallen left-half. In what way could he have been to blame for the inevitable?

The Victory lads were spurred on by this achievement and managed to have the upper hand for the remainder of the first half. When the whistle blew, Tommy's dad thrust a brown paper bag at Tommy and instructed him to attend to the players' needs. Needing no further invitation, Tommy raced onto the pitch to reach the team who had begun to congregate round their captain, awaiting the arrival of Mr Calvert to administer the interval mix of criticism, words of encouragement and pearls of wisdom designed to bring about the desired result at close of play.

Tommy presented the open bag to each player one by one, who then dipped in a hand which emerged clutching a quarter of an orange. These segments were transferred to panting mouths to be sucked at, chewed upon and regurgitated as flaccid peel, with the occasional pip spat out with some force.

None of this ritual was engaged in, however, by Jaffa or his brother Archie. They were busily occupied in benefiting from the restorative powers of a Capstan full strength each, ignited by a Swan Vesta – a box of which had mysteriously materialised, like the cigarette packet, from somewhere about Jaffa's person.

Tommy could only marvel at how he could have carried such provisions about him in the heat of battle, as well as gazing in awe at the contribution that this burning stick seemed to have towards the revitalisation of the two players. It seemed to do for them what the citrus juices and vitamins were doing for the rest of the team.

Soon enough, the ref blew his whistle vigorously amid a mini cloud of condensation to indicate that the teams should resume combat. The game followed pretty much the same pattern as the first half, with much straining of muscle and clouting of leather accompanied by loud exhortation and the not very occasional expletive.

In all this excitement, North Valley managed to score a second goal, only to have this advantage expunged by Victory's equaliser – a truly magnificent effort from their centre-half. It was a spectacular, if somewhat speculative, volley from well outside the area, not diminished in the slightest by the fortuitous deflection from his opposite number in the North Valley team.

This latter intervention ensured that the keeper was left clutching at the extremely thin air while the ball settled in the opposite corner of the goal. Well, it would have settled had the goalposts been adorned with nets, which of course they weren't. As a result, the shot clipped the top of the stone wall and soared on into the adjoining field, coming to rest finally in a neat pile of sheep droppings, from which Tommy ever so delicately extracted the ball with the tips of his fingers.

With the game restored and time moving on, Tommy looked around at the surrounding moorland hills whose summits were beginning to disappear in a veil of mist. It must be just about full-time. Then three short shrill blasts of the ref's whistle eventually signalled the end of the game with honours even at 2–2. It never ceased to amaze Tommy to see the opposing players who had jousted, sworn at, physically abused and even threatened each other walking off with handshakes and mutual back slapping. Why, one of the Victory players was even arranging to meet someone from the opposing team that very evening for a joint night out! What would the other factory lads make of that? As it happened – nothing! This seemed to be acceptable behaviour. Tommy was sure he wouldn't have done that in the same situation.

Kit bag, spare ball and assorted sporting detritus safely deposited in the car boot, it was time to clamber aboard and head for home. The players, still decorated with the stains of the afternoon's exertions, stiffly squeezed in alongside Tommy, who didn't mind at all being compressed up against the opposite door and window. He was satisfied enough being a part of the post-match reminiscences and receiving the occasional jibe and ruffling of his hair.

These were the comrades he would one day be sharing experiences with, just as soon as he was old enough to be able to kick the leather cannonball far enough to justify a place in the team.

Saturday Activities

Weekends came and went like fitful night-time clouds hiding and revealing the pallid winter moon, though to Tommy it seemed an age from one Saturday to the next. The ritual rarely varied.

Occasionally Mrs Calvert would have a clearout of the cupboards and drawers. This gave Tommy a task to which he submitted with mixed feelings. It was his job to tote the laden sack of assorted throw-out clothes to the ragman. While he hated the journey in case any of his pals should see him engaged in such humiliating labour, the sack wasn't very heavy, and in any case he could drag it along behind him. Keeping to the backstreets, he was usually able to avoid any embarrassing encounters and it only took about five minutes to reach the old mill several streets away.

Once safely inside the mill's old outer door, Tommy was able to relax and even enjoy the sensation of this strange environment. He first had to drag the sack up the narrow and well worn staircase with its sharp right turn. He inhaled the foisty but not unpleasant smell – a mixture of cotton, wood, machine oil and goodness knows what else that made up the atmosphere of the interior.

Pushing open the door at the top which admitted him to the heart of the business, Tommy limped in with his load, looking around for signs of life. He was greeted by the large figure of the ragman himself emerging from his dingy office, which was simply part of the mill floor with a small partition and doorway affording a little privacy and air of organisation.

"Put yer bag on them scales then, lad. What've you got in there?" enquired the ragman as if Tommy was aware of and responsible for its contents.

"Just some old clothes," replied Tommy, remembering just in time to add, "but there are some wool things in there." From previous visits, he knew that woollens fetched a better price than most other rags, though he'd no idea why.

The ragman separated the woollens and weighed them apart from the rest. Tommy never ceased to be fascinated by the large weigh scale with its crossbar and sliding counterbalance. The ragman seemed to only move the balance a fraction before screwing up his brow and making a quick calculation.

Thrusting his hand into the large pocket at the front of his apron, he emerged with a fistful of assorted coinage. From this hoard his other hand delicately extracted a few coins (Tommy could see at least one shiny silver one) and passed them over with a rather final, "There you go then, lad," which brought the transaction to an abrupt end.

Tommy retreated down the stairs rather more quickly than he had ascended and emerged onto the street to examine his earnings. There was a sixpence, a bronze threepenny piece and three larger copper coins. These amounted to eleven pence ha'penny; not quite a shilling and not as much as the last trip he had made to the mill. Was the ragman cheating his mum? I suppose the sack did feel lighter than the last time, thought Tommy, as he raced home clutching the profits.

Tiger the tabby was doing his tightrope impression along the top of the backyard gate as Tommy approached home. He waited until the cat's back feet had just made it to the top of the wall before he thumbed down the latch and flung open the gate.

Dad was just emerging from the coal shed when Tommy bounded into the yard. He muttered something about being careful when pushing open doors but whatever he said was lost to Tommy, as by then he was disappearing through the kitchen door. He was met by a cloud of steam as the washing boiler was in full production. Mrs Calvert held out her hand to see what Tommy had managed to earn. He proudly counted out the few coins into his Mum's red and wrinkled palm, whereupon she generously returned the three copper coins to Tommy as his reward for the trip.

Tommy gasped, "There's no need to pay me, Mum!" but he quickly realised that she considered the twopence ha'penny to be a legitimate and well earned part of his pocket money.

Once in his room, Tommy placed one of the pennies into his savings box and decided to use the other one and a half pennies for essential supplies – perhaps sweets or marbles or maybe some of each. Checking his box, he saw that he had managed to accumulate one shilling and seven pence ha'penny. Thus he was well on his way to achieving a budget to last him on his holidays when the family would be hiring a caravan on the Devon coast the following summer.

Lunch was the invariable heap of bacon sandwiches to be shared by the whole family, together with the plate of bacon crisps. These were the bacon rinds cut from the rashers and fried separately to provide a crunchy accompaniment to the delicious butties consisting of thick crusty bread dipped in the bacon fat and packed with steaming rashers. This was washed down with large cups of tea (a mug in Dad's case) and bread and marmalade if anyone was still hungry enough after the fried food. Tommy usually was, although he preferred strawberry jam to the rather bitter taste of the thick-cut marmalade which was the adults' favourite.

A quick wash and change, gathering up of the equipment and it was time once again to clamber into the Triumph saloon for another player round-up and to head off for the latest fixture, this time a home one on the large sloping fields near the park, which would be carpeted with leaves at this time of the year just to provide the players with a further test of their ball skills.

Tommy and his dad were home by 4:40 p.m., having dropped off the muddied team members who always enjoyed a lift home. Kick-off had been at 2 p.m. because of the fading winter daylight. This time the Victory team had managed a fairly comfortable 4–2 win. Tommy was thus looking forward to the sports report on the radio to find out if his teams had also managed a win.

With the radio tuned in and turned up so that everyone in the room could hear, the family – minus Shirley who was still out down town with her friends – settled round the table for the next regular Saturday meal ritual. This time the repast was potato cakes, lovingly prepared and hand-baked by Mum.

Her Saturday schedule was doing the family washing, followed by an afternoon in the kitchen up to her armpits in flour and the apparatus of meal preparation, which she seemingly took to with relish. Or was this just how it appeared to Tommy? Whatever the reason, Mum never seemed to complain and took great pleasure in seeing that her meals were so much appreciated. By the time the radio was singing out the familiar tune announcing the onset of the football results, Tommy's mouth was a mess of butter grease as he tucked into his second large potato cake.

He gulped down a hot mouthful just in time as the announcer intoned the critical words: "Football League Division One…" Along with his dad, Tommy liked to play the game of predicting the scores. This was done by awaiting the announcement of the home team's score and trying to forecast the opposing team's, with the help of the intonation of James Alexander Gordon.

This was not as difficult as it seemed, because he always gave a clue by raising or lowering the tone of his voice.

Thus, Tottenham Hotspur 2 (raised voice at end) might be followed by (low) Everton, which meant that they had obviously lost so could only have scored one or nil. Similarly, a raised voice for the latter team meant that the away team had won. This score was harder to predict as the winning margin could have been virtually anything. Draws were the easiest to get right because of the flat and level tone of the announcer, which almost seemed to infer that a draw was a boring result.

Pudding was a baked apple sponge, borne in from the kitchen by a steaming and still surprisingly cheerful Mum, bearing in mind her recent need to attend to her culinary duties in silence so as not to interrupt James Alexander's litany of results. This solemn ritual spanned the full gamut from the English First Division to the Third Division North and thence beyond to the outcomes of the Celtic struggles – even to "East Fife 3, Cowdenbeath 2."

Where on earth, or even whereabouts in Scotland, were these bastions of the noble game? Tommy had once tried unsuccessfully to ascertain from his rudimentary school atlas the precise locations of various Scottish stadia, but he had no success, even with Heart of Midlothian or Celtic and Rangers, although he could find Glasgow.

Not wanting any custard on his pudding – he had a deep loathing of the stuff from his experiences of school dinners – Tommy nevertheless risked a scalded mouth by bolting down the steaming sponge and baked apple. His father shook his head resignedly at the seeming indestructibility of his son's digestive organs.

Tommy promptly excused himself from the table, though Mum was just beginning her meal, and disappeared upstairs to his room. While he would soon be able to find out how his favourite teams' results affected their league standing in the following morning's paper, he needed to plot the Victory Works team's latest points onto the local paper's Amateur League Division One table for the previous week.

Of course, he couldn't tell if they had moved up or down or even stayed still until the other results were revealed next week, so it wasn't a very fruitful exercise but this didn't matter in the least to Tommy, who could gain hours of fun from simply looking at the other results in the league and finding out how Pendle Forest, Trawden, Bradley Mills and other local giants had fared. This was his football world, apart from the detached voice of James Alexander Gordon and the annual trip to the house of his dad's workmate. This was a treat afforded to him because this friend had a television and Tommy was invited to watch the Cup Final in May.

What a treat that was! Last year, Tommy remembered fondly, he was sitting glued to his chair next to his dad, listening enthralled to the sounds and commentary brought into their room courtesy of the airwaves. Their vivid, football-steeped imaginations would be put to use and serve to bring the occasion to life. In their mind's eye, the two of them would have no difficulty in conjuring up images of heroic sportsmen striding across the turf in muscle straining effort.

After each such listening, the tradition was for Tommy to race out onto the backstreets and perhaps meet with one or two other lucky lads. One of them would be responsible for the sudden materialisation of a plastic or rubber ball of approximate size. There would then follow a re-enactment of the salient moves and the goals from the final, irrespective of the outcome of the real thing. There were no prejudices. The boys were happy to worship every player on that great occasion, even if their adopted northern representatives had lost.

The Junior School

Regretfully, school life intruded upon these happy times, but in truth Tommy didn't mind attending St Joseph's junior and infants. At least he was an able pupil. Brains seemed to run in the family, and his older sister Shirley had been at the Convent secondary school for the last two and a bit years.

St Joseph's was about half a mile away from Tommy's house down a terraced street near to the town centre. The school building was not very distinguished, huddled as it was under the parish church of the same name which occupied the second floor of the large structure.

The stonework of this supposedly grand Edwardian structure, like that of all the other buildings in the area, was smutted by years of soot belched out from the myriad tall chimneys disgorging the waste from the weaving mill engine rooms. The charcoal pallor of the area was only relieved by the odd house front sporting a coat of whitewash or cream emulsion.

Tommy skipped cheerfully down Macleod Street, which led to the imposing double front doors of St Joseph's Church. As he went past the pocket-sized front gardens he allowed his arm to trail along the walls and occasional privet hedge which gave on to the pavement. He didn't seem affected by the odd whipping hedge twig which lashed and even scratched at the palm of his hand.

He paused to break off a leaf which he proceeded to carefully fold in two. This he held to his pursed lips and, blowing thereon, produced a fearful screeching note that faintly amused him, though not the old guy clutching a shopping bag who was at that moment emerging from a front doorway some eight yards distant. This was evident from the unfriendly scowl directed at Tommy, who appeared not to notice. Indeed, why should he have, because the young lad was on a different planet altogether from the old chap.

In fact, Tommy had just noticed his classmate Stella (one of the nicer looking girls in the school – not that Tommy was interested) approaching from the opposite direction. The two of them met almost simultaneously at the unprepossessing gateway alongside the church front.

This gateway – it had long ceased to possess an actual gate – gave on to the school playground, which was bounded on the one side by a high wall and the priest's house and on the other by the school and church itself. Well, bounded was not quite the most accurate description for the latter two-storey structure. It positively loomed over the playground, effectively blanketing out the sun and casting a large shadow over much of the yard for a considerable part of the year. This of course meant that in the frozen depths of winter, the surface of the yard resembled not so much a playground as the petrified surface of a brooding lake.

Tommy still sensed the echo of a hard lump on the back of his skull which had reared up as a result of his legs giving way and dumping him on his noggin during a particularly frosty November morning. He didn't even get much sympathy, let alone any time off school. Still, he should have been grateful for the brisk way in which his injury was remedied by the petite but wiry Miss Ratcliffe of junior 3. She it was who happened to be the first responsible person on the scene, being as how she was on playground duty at the time. She had marched him unceremoniously into the boys' toilets, there to apply a cold compress of soaked toilet paper to the back of Tommy's head. He could still wince even after several weeks at the thought of her "delicate" nursing that day.

Tommy and Stella strolled into the playground happily chatting away until, and then, as if by some preordained signal, they parted – Stella to join the small group of girls who had already gathered there and Tommy to race over to his mate Noel who was enthusiastically bashing a rubber ball at the wall with vigorous swings of his right boot. A shout of surprise and annoyance burst from Noel's mouth as Tommy raced off with the ball.

"Come back 'ere, you little Arab," yelled Noel, who proceeded to chase after his ball.

Tommy sought refuge behind the girls, much to their disgust, which increased when Noel swung around the outermost girl to get at his opponent and in the process succeeded in dumping her on the hard floor. Any further altercation was rendered impossible, for at that moment the air was rent by the strident clanging of the school bell. This was being rung (or was it wrung?) by its namesake, the amply built Mrs Bell of junior 2. She stood majestically at the top of the short flight of steps that led up to the school from the yard itself.

Before the last peal of the bell had dissipated in the clear morning air the children had begun to shuffle obediently into their lines. One prolonged glare from Ma Bell and the shuffling and whispering transformed into silent and quite orderly ranks of pupils, albeit with the odd dripping nose and heavy exhalation of breath, the latter mostly from the more tardy arrivals who had broken into a run on hearing the clanging noise as they approached the gateway.

Once inside the central school space – which saw life as hall, PE space and, in turn, dining room – the eight lines of children – two for each junior class, one of boys, one of girls – became a sea of faces. These, some grinning, some agape and some downright nervous, gazed up at their nemesis in the shape of Mr Tarmey.

Mr Tarmey (or Old Barmy Tarmey, as the children were wont, on careful and secret occasion, to christen him) stared back in turn. His gimlet eye seemed to reach into the soul of each child who dared to look back, as if seeking therein some inkling of a confession.

In truth, Tarmey's beady eyes weren't nearly as effective as the children feared they were. Though they sparkled with maliciousness, at distances greater than fifteen feet their view of the world was decidedly misty and lacking in sharp detail. Thus they were quite incapable of spotting any sly winks or grins from the top dogs of junior 4 in the back rows. Not that even the boldest of them would attempt anything untoward, flanked as they were by their form teacher, Mr Dickson, on the right and the equally formidable aforementioned Miss Ratcliffe on the other side.

It was Miss Ratcliffe who held the honour of being Tommy's class teacher. Well, he wasn't the sole object of her dedicated ministry. Tommy shared that privilege with the other thirty-two young souls in Junior 3 – eighteen boys and fifteen girls to be precise. There weren't really many budding geniuses in this group, if any at all, but rarely did any child in the class give much less than one hundred per cent of his or her best.

This situation was made possible by a combination of a strange feeling of affection for Miss R and a healthy respect for her left arm which, at full stretch, could deliver a most effective and sharp reminder to the rear of one's skull that obedience and concentration were the least that she could expect from her dears.

Still, each child remembered fondly, that was preferable to close proximity in the company of their previous class teacher, Mrs Bell. This was not so much for fear of her as for sheer nausea at the pungent aroma emitted by said lady. Tommy could still remember the hour endured by him last year when he had had the misfortune to be seated next to her on the pew in church. He thought at the time that he might even pass out, so overcome was he by her aura. And he thought ladies were supposed to at least smell nice – that is if they spent even half the time that his sister did on their ablutions and beauty preparations.

Such musings on his time at St Joseph's were abruptly snuffed out by the strident notes escaping from the piano, which reeled under the hammer blows of Ma Bell's energetic fingers as she subjected the keys to a merciless assault. It was time to heed the urgent demand from Mr Tarmey to, "Sing up now everyone – you all know this hymn!"

Do we? thought Tommy irrelevantly as he too began at first to mime and then caterwaul the words of the exhortation to all the saints, gradually matching the lyrics to the tune in some semblance of order if not of timing.

Prayers followed hymn, announcements followed prayer and with final exhortations from Mr Tarmey to all and sundry to work hard and behave – or else, it was time to dismiss. This meant a retreat behind the wood and glass partitions which demarcated each of the four classrooms, there to spend endless hours calculating, matriculating and scribing. Still, at least you got to mostly sit down on your own separate chair, sharing two to a double desk. In the lower junior classes they still had the unyielding bench seats attached to the desks. The privileges of age! thought Tommy.

It was the arithmetic lesson. Tommy didn't mind this as he was skilfully numerate and thus adept at the laborious but basically straightforward arithmetical calculations that were spread before the class. Not so with Brenda, the sturdily built girl with whom Tommy, to his great mortification, was obliged to share a desk.

She had not managed to earn many of the sugar cubes awarded by Mrs Bell last year to all those pupils who mastered each times table up to 12 x 12. Furthermore, she seemed to have difficulty even adding a string of unit numbers, let alone knowing how to carry to the tens column. Brenda was therefore obliged to indulge in subterfuge. She mastered the art of leaning back ever so slightly so that she could peer at the answers that Tommy had arrived at with ease.

It was some time before she was rumbled, and not even then by Miss Ratcliffe. It took Tommy some time to realise how Brenda always seemed to manage good scores in her arithmetic when she was clearly a struggler. Blooming cheek! It was one thing to help a mate who was stuck, but fancy nicking all his answers without having the decency to ask!

It didn't take Tommy long to find a way out of this situation, not that he would have told the teacher. After all, one drew the line at snitching to them! A devious but nonetheless effective strategy soon brought about a solution to the problem.

During the next few arithmetic lessons, Tommy worked out the answers to his sums and didn't take much care over concealing them from Brenda. She in turn would eagerly transfer these onto her own sums.

The devious part came next. Tommy would take considerable time over the last sum and then peer at his work as if double-checking the answers. They were good enough for Brenda though, and on completion of the last crib, she couldn't wait to hurry out to Miss Ratcliffe's desk to have them marked.

At that point Tommy would revisit his answers and carefully change the odd digit – a 0 would become a 6, a 1 change into a 7 and so on. He would then join the queue for marking – he was usually one of the first out but never mind – and there he would gaze innocently at the ceiling whilst awaiting his turn.

Upon returning to his desk with his best work suitably adorned with rows of ticks, he would sidle back alongside the crestfallen Brenda who was by now close to tears and racked with the problem of doing her corrections. She couldn't understand this. Surely she had copied down Tommy's answers correctly? Usually he was so reliable and anyway, he seemed on this occasion to have his work all correct! Of course she couldn't say a thing and from then on she desisted from copying, relying instead on her own far from secure numerical aptitude.

Playtime witnessed a mad dash, from the boys at least, to the outside roofless urinals to gain blessed relief before emerging onto the playground for re-enactments of the Indian Wars, Second World War battles (German or Japanese) or simply good old-fashioned "tig".

It never ceased to fascinate Tommy whenever he happened to come across young Bulcock during his mad careering around the yard. Whereas the other lads made do with no sustenance other than perhaps the odd surplus boiled sweet stuck to the lining of their pockets, this posh kid had an orange and a bar of chocolate. Not only that, he even consumed these with an affected air. He would wander around the yard, oblivious to other company – maybe he didn't want to share – dipping his chocolate bar into a juicy half orange and then sucking the result with obvious relish. Ah well, if that made him happy. Personally Tommy would sooner have his mates than luxury grub if it came accompanied with loneliness.

Lunchtime – school dinner – was eagerly awaited by some souls but not Tommy. While there were children in the school who clearly were underfed and undernourished at home, Tommy was thankfully not one of these unfortunate souls. While his general appearance did nothing to distinguish him from most of his peers, clad as they all were in the standard "uniform" of shirt, short flannel trousers and vary coloured jumpers – print dresses and cardigans in the case of the girls – the clue was in the faces.

All the children bore ravages of their existence in the form of spots, crooked teeth, squinty eyes and temporary scars, scabs and wounds that were the result of their rough and lively play. These blemishes were quite the norm. What distinguished the undernourished ones were the gaunt expressions in their eyes, which lacked a little of the usual sparkle and had a slightly haunted quality about them.

Having jostled for the obligatory hand scrubbing in the narrow and cold space of the toilet blocks with their wet, bare wooden floors and smell of disinfectant and carbolic, the children shuffled eagerly (or reluctantly) into some semblance of order to queue outside the dining "hall". This was the same general purpose area which had served for assembly and would become the PE gym in the afternoon. In the meantime it had been transformed by caretaker and dinner ladies into a communal dining area. The large aluminium tins containing the dish of the day had been transferred with much puffing and panting from the Education Authority delivery van, which had arrived from the central kitchens.

There being insufficient room for all the children to eat in the main hall, Tommy's class was designated to eat in junior 2 classroom. Patrick, the bespectacled tall lad who had taken a liking to Tommy, beckoned to Tommy to join him at the double desk in the third row. The two of them settled down to await the culinary treat.

Tommy turned round to check his surroundings and was met by the grinning face of Brenda – she of the arithmetic cribbing – and her friend Rita. Obviously she had not taken too much offence over her earlier humiliation.

Oh, well, it takes all sorts, ruminated Tommy, as he turned round to be met head on by the looming and florid face of one of the dinner ladies. She presented him with a large plateful of semi-warm food as if she were laying an array of exotic jewels before a potentate. Tommy glanced down to see the realisation of his worst fears. It was meat (animal origin unknown) swimming in lukewarm gelatinous gravy, sharing a bed with boiled white cabbage and a large potato similarly maltreated.

His Adam's apple positively quivered as he gave a huge gulp at the prospect of having to consume this mess. As he glanced to his right, he saw that Jimmy Johnson had already made large inroads into his portion and was apparently downing the rest with great relish. What on earth did that lad usually have to contend with as a source of nourishment?

There was no time for further conjecture on this topic. Tommy had to force down as much of the menu as he could face without risking an attack of nausea before aforesaid dinner lady came for his plate. He managed a heroic effort of clearing three-quarters of his share, aided by the strategy of offloading most of his cabbage onto Jimmy's eagerly proffered plate.

This considerable achievement was wiped from the face of both Tommy and Patrick when they were promptly presented with a deep bowl each. These contained their "pudding", which would have done justice as freight ballast, consisting as it did of a large wedge of sponge surrounded by custard with a thicker skin than the gravy could boast of. It would have earned the title of "spotted dick" had it contained more than one currant.

The consumption of this dubious delight presented a mild challenge to Patrick. It brought out a cold sweat on Tommy, for he loathed custard. How he loathed the stuff! He had never been able to face it since the day he was virtually force-fed it in the infant class. Manfully he took generous bite-sized chunks of the bland sponge cake, carefully avoiding undue contact with the stuff of his nightmares.

His luck was in this time! Taking advantage of the momentary distraction of the forceful dinner lady, who was busy mopping up a spillage of her precious custard from the floor, he seized the moment and scooped the remains of his pudding into the slop bucket.

Afternoon was nature study – that wonderfully inspiring and absorbing communion with the beauty of British fauna, or it would have been if there were available any more interesting resources than the faded black and white illustrations and boring script contained within the well worn cover of the standard textbook.

The children would possibly have been more motivated had they been taken to observe at close hand even some of the local dandelions which sprouted around every corner and plot of spare ground, or sampled a few choice rhubarb stalks burgeoning in many allotments in the area. However, Miss Ratcliffe had absolutely no intention of venturing outside the closet comfort of her classroom with her eager brood.

Salvation, and with it fresh air, came after playtime when it was the games lesson. The girls would remain confined within the high walls of the playground for whatever games girls played. Certainly there were no netball posts or any other such grand equipment at St Joseph's – only the large wire baskets containing an assortment of ropes, quoits and skittles (wooden) with the occasional ball that perhaps may not be too deflated to prevent worthwhile use.

Mr Dickson and the boys required only one large football (worn leather, faded and loose stitched) and whatever each child chose to wear. It was too cold to allow for the stripped down appearance of vests, short pants and bare feet which was the norm for indoor PE. After all, they had to trek down Victoria Street, over the canal bridge and past the back wall of the weaving sheds in order to reach the municipal playing field adjacent to Victoria Park. Those boys fortunate enough to own football boots, and their number included Tommy, either wore them strung round their necks by the laces or carried them in hand.

As if to order, each pair of boys broke rank as they crossed the canal bridge to hoist themselves up and to peer over the parapet in the hope of seeing something of interest within the rainbow-slicked and murky surface water. Nothing doing, unless a few spars of broken crate or an old pram hood counted. Certainly no barge had disturbed these waters for many a year. Even the mill's defunct loading door and bay which backed onto the water spoke of neglect, although the mill was still a going concern.

Tommy thought briefly of his mother who would at that very moment be busily occupied controlling the working of the several looms allocated to her in Bradley's mill just half a mile away. He was once allowed into the cacophony of her working environment. He would never forget the awesome banging din of a hundred or more weaving looms with their incessantly clattering shuttles which rendered audible speech useless. How on earth did his mum and the other women manage to endure it day after day?

Patrick's nose flattened abruptly on the shoulder of the boy in front as he was busy chatting to Tommy and hadn't noticed that Mr Dickson had halted the lines. They had reached the games field at last. There was a brief pause while the hardiest among them removed their pullovers and flung them to the long grass at the side of the pitch. Tommy took his off also, not because he was immune to the chill air but in order to avoid the wrath of Mrs Calvert should his pullover get damaged in any way. Once the high-sided brown boots with their iron-hard toecaps had been tugged on, Mr Dickson announced start of play by giving the football a hefty hoof into the blue. It was instantly pursued by a mob of junior 3 and 4 boys, each one eager to get in the first kick or perhaps wrap their hands around it and thus claim rights to the legal kick-off.

The next twenty minutes of the "game" followed a similar format to the opening hoof but on a children's scale, interspersed with the occasional peep of Mr D's acme thunderer. There was certainly no pattern to the play, let alone any inkling of positional strategy from the boys. In this sense it bore a closer resemblance to the medieval version than anything engaged in by professional players on Saturday afternoons. No matter; it served to dissipate the pent-up energy of twenty-nine boys who had been cooped up with their manuals of British flora for the previous hour.

May

M ay had begun with a delightful warm spell which banished the chill memories of winter and served to remind everyone of the promise of long, blissful evenings, holidays and endless lines of washing or endless hours of play, depending on one's daily lot.

The football season had all but drawn to a close. Once more, Tommy's beloved team had found themselves marooned in mid-table with no hope of glory this year, having been knocked out of the FA Cup in the fourth round. Still, there was the chance to cheer on a northern team in the Cup Final as Preston were to compete with West Brom.

Before the promise of that particular football feast, there was a need within Tommy to get the feel of the forthcoming summer bliss with its long school holidays stretching ahead. So it was that Tommy set out on a particularly sunny Saturday morning with the sole aim of heading for the top end of town, if only to create the illusion of escaping into the verdant countryside. Before long he found that he had reached the top of Railway Street. It was only another ten-minute walk to reach Marsden Park, and he hadn't been there since last autumn.

That occasion didn't really count anyway, as he had driven there with Dad to see the Victory football team. This time he would walk right through the park itself. Thus he strolled with frequent upward glances to the tops of the huge trees which towered above the asphalt path and manicured lawns. Skirting the ranks of the equally impressive rhododendrons with their masses of pink and purple bloom, he turned toward the large pond.

Tommy paused to peer at the mirrored surface and was met with a dazzling reflective glare which bored into the eyes. Turning his neck and at the same time shielding his eyes, he could just pick out the clusters of ducks mustering in the shaded parts of the lake. Nearer the middle, the mirror was shattered by a multiple vee of ripples, at the narrowed end of which glided a pair of magnificent swans. These graceful creatures fascinated Tommy, not least because of the tales he had heard of their ability to break a man's arm with the beat of a wing. Why would such graceful creatures want to do that anyway? he mused. When he grew bored with watching the antics of the various water fowl, Tommy decided to head for the hothouse.

Marsden Park had a particularly splendid conservatory of exotic plants which were nurtured through the coldest seasons by means of large heating pipes that encircled the bedding sections. Being very mindful of preserving the ambience, Tommy opened and then carefully closed behind him the outer door.

As soon as he pushed open the inner door, Tommy's nostrils took in the wonderful aroma of warm damp soil and that peculiar "green" smell that only succulent plants and a hothouse atmosphere could engender. Even the gravel pathway and crafted stonework walls seemed imbued with the scent. Tommy breathed in blissfully and listened to the gentle music of the water fountain feature which sparkled in the centre. It was easy to imagine that one was standing in a tropical forest paradise, which was probably why the hothouse appealed so much to Tommy.

He began his tour of the house, pausing every two or three steps to gaze in fascination at each display of greenery. He had no idea what the plants were, but they conjured up visions of hot and steaming locations and equatorial splendour, the likes of which he had only read about in adventure comics and tales of great exploration that he had eagerly digested from books borrowed from the local children's library.

He sat awhile on the edge of the warm stone surround to the fountain, trailing his fingers in the run-off pool and listening to the tune of the gurgling waters.

After about twenty minutes of this blissful solitude, Tommy's peace was shattered by an elderly couple obviously like minded to enjoy the scene themselves. That was Tommy's signal to depart. The spell was broken and anyway it must be near lunchtime, or so his stomach suggested.

The following Saturday was the Cup Final itself – the biggest game in the whole season. Up to now, Tommy had spent this particular afternoon each year sat at the dining table with his dad for as long as he could remember. The pair of them would sit spellbound, listening to the sounds from Wembley brought into their home by the radiogram.

The female members of the family made themselves scarce on this occasion; Mum retiring to the kitchen to wash, scrub, bake and generally occupy herself with whatever mums found to do in their domain. Shirley took even more drastic action, leaving the house to go "down town" with her friends.

This particular year, though, brought even more joy to Tommy. Dad's pal at work had bought a television and had invited them to join him for the occasion. Much to Tommy's puzzlement, Dad declined, preferring to listen at home. However, he did arrange that Tommy could go round to Mr Wallwork's house to *see* the Cup Final! Thus it was that at 2.20 p.m. on the Saturday, Tommy was seated on the carpet in Mr W's house, his back to the arm of the settee. The grown-ups, four men and two women, occupied all the seats within viewing range of the ten-inch screen.

I bet the women are only here because it's a TV, thought a disgusted Tommy, and they won't know who the teams are. This was at least partly true, judging by the questions they kept firing at the men until shushed into silence before kick-off. Tommy watched mesmerised. Up till now, he had had to visualise the scenes brought to him via the airwaves. Now it was all before him, and very much as he had imagined it would be – but so much better.

Panoramic sweeping shots of the crowd with their rosettes and rattles, interviews with various notables and outside the ground with fans, close-ups of programme sellers, police and bandsmen – it was all there in vivid grey and white. Tommy watched unblinkingly and oblivious to his increasingly numbed bottom on the hard carpet.

There was the conductor in his splendid white suit, standing proudly on his podium and leading band and crowd alike in the community singing. Among the chosen songs was a rendition of "Lassie from Lancashire" in honour of the county's representatives in the Final. After "I Love to Go A-Wandering" was bellowed out by a hundred thousand fans and fifty or so guardsmen, it was time for the perennially popular and moving "Abide With Me".

The two teams emerged together into the sunshine stride by stride to a crescendo of roars, screams and clapping. The royal walk, introductions, handshakes and limbering up passed in an instant and Mrs Wallwork had just time to present Tommy with a glass of orange (the adults were taking tea) as the referee blew for the captains to converge in order to toss the coin.

West Bromwich Albion kicked off to a tremendous wave of sound, added to by the men in the room "shushing" the two women into reverential silence. While the adults in the sitting room passed sundry comments with regard to the match and the performance of both players and referee, Tommy watched in spellbound awe and silence. How majestic were these heroic figures who strode the turf so lustily and smote both ball and opposing players with a fervour.

This was football *par excellence*, so different from the game of the same name enacted by the Victory team and their opponents on the local playing fields. But these were professionals, the *crème de la crème*, after all! Not that Tommy was familiar with such soubriquets, but he could appreciate quality when he witnessed it for himself.

Mrs Wallwork duly handed round cups of tea and short-bread biscuits during the half-time interval. The menfolk came alive and engaged in animated discussion on the performances of both teams and the referee. There was much enthusing about the efforts of Preston North End and their prospects of victory. Most of this passed quite literally over Tommy's head.

He was enthralled with the marching band, especially when it changed direction – the perfectly straight lines of busby-headed soldiers wheeling about through a hundred and eighty degrees and returning unerringly through their rear ranks whilst maintaining the tempo and tune of each stirring air. They were still marching off the pitch when the returning players emerged to resume combat. This was the signal for the menfolks' chatter to gradually subside until, by the time that the referee was poised with whistle in mouth, utter silence had once again descended on the Wallwork lounge.

The second half was a blur of end-to-end activity, but seemingly the team from the Midlands were beginning to assert themselves and according to the consensus in the sitting room might even make a comeback and steal the game. So it proved to be. To the disappointment of the televiewers, Preston couldn't hang on. Everyone had rooted for them of course, because they were the northern team and what's more were Lancashire's own. But it wasn't to be their day and the Albion took the match, and thus the FA Cup itself, by three goals to two.

All too soon the presentations were over for another year. After mumbling a grateful thanks to his hosts, Tommy dashed away and back to his house. He grabbed his football, raced out again, and sprinted up the street to call on Robert and whoever else he could contact. Eventually there were four of them in all and the ritual was the same as per previous Cup Finals.

Two of them would be North End and the others West Brom. Then, once more, the Cup Final would be played over again. No matter what the outcome this time, it was accepted that at least some of the finer moments from the match would be re-enacted on the backstreet between Camden and Beaufort Streets.

The third Saturday in May was as enshrined in the local calendar with no less status than the Cup Final. It was Nelson Gala Day. On this day, come rain or shine, everyone (it seemed) from miles around either took part in or witnessed this splendid event. Tommy was a lucky boy, for his mother was a part-time waitress at the Lord Nelson Hotel. This meant that he had access to the hotel balcony which looked out on to Manchester Road. This was a prime location, for didn't the gala procession route take it right past the front of the hotel?

Mrs Calvert made sure that Tommy was granted a spot on the balcony by 12.30. She would be busy serving the lunchtime clientele for at least the next hour but Tommy was assured of a grandstand view of the proceedings, which were scheduled to kick off at 1.30. Sure enough, he could hear the distant sound of the leading brass band carried on the breeze just about on time. First in view was the mayoral procession, a rather uninteresting cavalcade of limousine and walking dignitaries.

Then came the real parade! First there was a resplendent military band followed by the glamorous sight of ranks of

Morris dancing girls. How smart they looked in their colourful, be-ribboned tunics and skirts. Many of them were weighed down with gleaming banks of medals, whilst at their head high-stepped the leading girl, who twirled and threw her baton with consummate skill. Tommy had little time for the girls in school but, although he wouldn't admit it to even his closest pal, he was in love with these splendid specimens.

Tommy was to enjoy the sight of five more teams of these girls, each company in its own livery just like football teams. Then there were the floats. How imaginatively the local firms and shops had prepared these. Ordinary flat-back lorries had been transformed into wonderful stages of fantasy. There were May Queens, fairytale pageants, Wild West panoramas, underwater realms, military parades and historical tapestries – every one a delight of coloured bunting, wonderful costume and creative camouflaging of the wagons. All this complete with weirdly costumed figures walking alongside the wagons and encouraging the crowd to throw coins into their buckets. There were yet more bands – brass, pipe and drum – and files of marching scouts, guides and war veterans. There were cars, old and new and all shining brightly, each one occupied by several unknown people, all keen to add to the occasion by waving vigorously to the crowds.

The entire procession must have lasted at least three-quarters of an hour, by which time Mrs Calvert and the other hotel staff had pressed onto the balcony to witness the splendour. Tommy's mum managed to press a glass of fruit squash, "borrowed" no doubt from the lunch trolley, into Tommy's hand. He gratefully quaffed the cool, sweet juice before focussing his attention once more on the seemingly endless cavalcade.

After an age of this visual feast had taxed the concentration of the watchers on the balcony and several of the crowd who had begun to edge away, the parade was eventually whittled down to a few bedraggled, and no doubt tired, marchers at the rear. They would follow the whole down Carr Road to the gala site at Victoria Park, where the festivities would continue for another hour or so.

Tommy was well pleased. He had seen the entire procession in comfort from a splendid and unencumbered viewpoint. He was ready for home and the teatime potato pancakes, even if there was no sports report and football results service now that the season had finished.

The final Saturday in May brought with it another regular ritual. It was matinee morning at the pictures. This wasn't actually a weekly event now that several households had a television set. There may have been nothing on the little screen at that time of day, but many parents would be blowed if they were going to cop up for the price of a cinema ticket for their little dears as well as the cost of the TV rental.

However, enough mums and dads *had* come up with the readies to ensure that several members of the gang could make their way down to the Alhambra for the morning performance. Those who couldn't get their parents to cough up had used their paper round money or had run errands for generous neighbours.

This morning's show was a triple bill. There was excitement, adventure and comedy. The five lads, Tommy among them, shuffled past the kiosk, sliding their carefully counted entrance money through the grille. They skipped down the dark and dusty aisle and flung themselves into some seats about halfway to the screen and fairly near the middle. The auditorium was filling up fast. It was a good job they had come early. The noise gradually grew in volume until it became a hubbub of laughter, whistles, shouts and shuffling.

This miraculously died down as the lights dimmed and the curtains began to withdraw to the sides to reveal a huge screen emblazoned with the opening credits. Actually, these had already begun to project on to the curtains in order to quell the cacophony. A reverential hush descended, broken only by the occasional ignorant catcall.

First up was the comedy: Larry, Curly and Mo, otherwise known as the "Three Stooges". Their forte was to get themselves into deep water and regale the audience with their comic antics in dealing with their predicament. Fast-talking and much slapstick was the fare, and it seemed to be appreciated by most of the young audience, though the performance did not enhance itself in Tommy's view. He preferred a little less farce and a little more subtlety.

On the face of it, the next film did not promise to deliver the goods. However, it was all about Tommy's favourite scenario – the Wild West. Cowboys and Indians, or in this case cowboys and "baddies", was a sure-fire script. It had everything to fire a young boy's imagination – stagecoaches, cattle, ranch houses, saloons and heroes and villains to match.

There were immaculately turned out cattle ranchers (doubling as the posse), dubious bad men complete with beard growth and bandannas and, almost inevitably, Tom Mix as the hero of the hour. Tommy saw nothing even faintly ridiculous about his oversized white Stetson – a "ten gallon" hat if ever there was one.

There was a hold-up, a kidnap (complete with helpless female victim), a prolonged chase and a shoot-out.

The auditorium rang to the whoops and cheers, with occasional jeers, of the young cinemagoers. How they lapped it up as the posse chased the badmen along the trail, around the trees and among the rocks. The fact that they seemed to pass the same background several times during the course of the pursuit somehow eluded the audience, so caught up were they in the thrill of the chase.

Shots banged out from revolvers, puffs of gunsmoke wafted on the air and howls of pain erupted from the badmen's ranks. Several of them fell without any visible sign of bloodshed, which would have been hard to detect in black and white anyway. The miscreants, what were left of them, were duly rounded up and returned to justice. Tom Mix's posse of course suffered no serious casualties. Well, they did have justice on their side after all.

As the curtain came down on this frenzy of activity, bodies leapt up from cinema seats to make an emergency dash to the toilet, to join the queue for refreshments or just to stretch saddle sore limbs. The usherette, who had stealthily tiptoed down the aisle complete with torch during the climax of the action, was inundated. Eager hands thrust coppers and silver into her palm in exchange for bars of chocolate, plastic drinks and tubs of ice cream.

Tommy, who had remained chair bound, watched as Ronnie flung himself back into the adjacent seat with his prizes. Under the seat went his Kia-Ora orange squash and straw while he tackled his Fry's chocolate cream bar.

"How much did those cost?" gasped an amazed Tommy.

"Oh, I dunno, about one and threepence," shrugged a nonchalant Ronnie.

Tommy watched him demolish the chocolate bar. No chance of a piece of that, then. At least he got some entertainment from watching Ronnie's jaws at work. He sat fascinated at the sight of the wrinkles on the side of Ronnie's head every time he chewed.

I never thought the side of someone's head moved like that whenever he was eating, he mused to himself. Oh, well, it's time for the last part of the show.

The lights had slowly dimmed, catching out the latecomers who had to scramble back into their seats on returning from the toilets. The dramatic music had commenced. With a rising tide of noise enveloping the excited rabble, the large screen blazed out the huge lettering announcing the adventures of – Flash Gordon!

Waves of cheering broke and subsided during the overture and subtitles before shushing and nudging reduced the throng to a reverent hush.

There was Flash, in his immaculate silver spacesuit, conferring with his crew and superiors. Much high-pitched, animated discussion took place before the intrepid team set off to confront the evils of the universe.

There was the spectacular rocket with its unique take-off manoeuvre. This consisted of a climbing spiral with humming engines and much sparking of exhausts. They were off to face unknown dangers on Planet X.

Tommy, being a seasoned veteran of the space exploits of Mr Gordon, knew what lay in store. These were his favourite baddies – the Clay Men. They were particularly malevolent because of their fiendish camouflage. While the unsuspecting Flash and friends were exploring the surroundings, the Clay Men melted (literally) into the rocks and cliff faces, only to emerge and metamorphose while the heroes' backs were turned.

It took all the frantic screaming and yelling of the watchers to alert Flash and company to the danger in time to save their skins.

Exit doors were flung open, allowing the sunlight to burst in and the crowds of boys and girls to surge out onto the backstreet. The show was over for another week, but many of them would see the Clay Men once more in their disturbed dreams as they again fused into and melted out of solid rock.

Expedition to Pendle

It was one of those all too infrequent balmy spells of clear sunny weather that inspired the lads of the locality to make plans for a grand expedition. This climatic bonus had arrived none too soon, coming after several days of dreary cloud and persistent drizzle which had driven a desperate Tommy to seek amusement indoors. This was never a favoured option, as it meant endless games of football or battles re-enacted on the lounge carpet using his large collection of buttons. It was quite intriguing how the lad's ingenuity had, with the aid of a small simulated pearl ball and a die, managed to transform these haberdashery items into competing football teams or rival armies.

Many a dull hour had passed more easily when Tommy's imagination had got to work on these scenarios. Mum had put a stop to the balloon football game that Tommy had played out in the living room, for fear of injury to the ornaments – not to mention the family cat.

Anyway, such diversions were banished from the agenda for the present, thanks to the upturn in the weather and the aforementioned plans. It was during a serious discussion on the garden wall of the local chippy that Brian had come up with the inspirational suggestion. How long was it since any of them had climbed Pendle Hill? Come to that, had some of those present *ever* climbed it to the top before? Oh, they were all well acquainted with the brooding presence of the magnificent dark ridge of moorland, what with the fact that it loomed over the local towns and it was after all steeped in the timeless mystery of witchcraft. It may well be over three miles from their neighbourhood to the base of Pendle, but that was as nothing to a group of footloose and intrepid boys with time to kill on their endless summer holidays.

So it was that, in several households in the Camden Street area, young lads (tongues curled outside lips in concentration) were busy preparing essential provisions for the expedition. Watched over by patient mums, exasperated paters and sometimes scoffing elder siblings, the expedition members set about the task of cutting and buttering thick wedges of white bread prior to ladling jam, syrup or other unhealthy but nourishing fillings onto their surfaces.

Occasionally and in the less adventurous households, an over-indulgent mum would brush aside her little darling and, much to the latter's disgust, insist upon putting up a "proper" lunch that would sustain her hero throughout the day.

Those who, like Tommy, were allowed to determine their own survival were busy filling empty pop bottles with all manner of desirable nectar from Spanish water (if previously and surreptitiously brewed by those with foresight) to blackcurrant cordial or even Tizer or Dandelion and Burdock. Of course, the hardier souls would suffice with water, though Tommy couldn't later recall seeing anyone partaking of this spartan fare.

Sleep did not come easily to any of the expedition members, partly because of the sultry night but more to do with their mounting excitement. Nevertheless, they met as pre-arranged at 8.30 a.m. outside old Atkins' newsagents. Ronnie and Robert had already stocked up from the chewing gum machine on the wall, Robert even gaining the extra free pack on the fourth turn of the knob.

So it was with uplifted spirits that they set off down town and downhill, chattering and striding out at a pace that would never be sustained. The group gradually formed into pairs for the practicalities of following the pavement and at least resembling in appearance the armed expeditionary patrol that they quite clearly had become. The troop soon passed Manchester Road, descended Carr Road and crossed the canal bridge, which led them towards Victoria Park and the edge of town.

Now the trek became serious. They were leaving familiar places behind and entering "the real countryside". Somehow, even though none could admit that he had trod this particular path, they collectively and instinctively knew that the right of way they were following would lead them to their destination, for any view of Pendle was obliterated by the much closer upward facing valley side which was on their route.

The last abodes and gardens soon gave way to emerald green undulating pastures bounded by rickety stone walls. Their path, worn partly to moist bare soil by countless predecessors, weaved steadily uphill roughly parallel to the up-reaching stone walls and skirting occasional cow pats, cairns of sheep droppings and outcrops of thistles. Already the boys were inhaling exaggerated breaths of the pleasantly cool air and proclaiming how invigorating it was.

Talk became fitful – lung power was needed for the more essential task of providing energy to power their leg muscles. Actually, they were all fit lads and carried no surplus body weight, thanks to their regular routine of outdoor play at every opportunity. Even Brian, large by the standards of the group, was not considered to be at all fat but merely an imposing figure, which no doubt helped him achieve some status in the group. He was some nine months older than most of the others and this fact too lent him an air of authority.

Before long they were well up the valley side and able to look down upon the shrinking panorama of Nelson. They could take in almost the whole sweep of the town – the mill chimneys, central clock tower, church spires and the taller municipal and industrial structures which rose above their humbler surrounds.

It was Tony who broke the rest break by declaring that he could be first to reach the first staging post at the summit of the hill. He made this pronouncement after ensuring that he had stolen a twenty yard lead on the backward glancing group. This served to animate the rest of them into a baying mob that set off in hot pursuit of its quarry.

Thus they arrived hot and breathless at Noggarth Top. Here was salvation for the parched crew in the form of the single-storey cottage which occupied the point at which field path met the tarmac of the road at its bend before the descent into the hamlet of Roughlee. The salvation came in the form of the little shop and café which was run by the owners and which catered for the weary foot traveller or infrequent motorist.

Those blessed with spending money bestowed by over-indulgent parents surged into the shop to clamour for iced lollies, fizzy pop and sweet confections. They were swiftly rounded up into some semblance of order by the proprietor, a gangly beanpole of a man who nevertheless had the air of a Scout troop leader. With cheerful aplomb but authoritative voice he subdued the eager crew until each member had dutifully requested his particular needs.

One by one the shoppers emerged clutching an ice cream cone, a paper bag of sweets or a bottle of pop – two or three items for the greedier. The hardier and more disciplined contented themselves with resting on the two wooden forms, unscrewing bottle tops and swigging blissful mouthfuls of their precious rations. By common consent, none reached for his sandwich pack. It would be suicide to indulge in the one and only meal at such an early stage. It was still only mid-morning, certainly not yet eleven.

The weak ones who had given in to temptation, and who anyway had too much surplus cash, felt obliged to excuse their indulgence by offering some of their provender to their companions. This was of course dutifully accepted and after much rustling and rummaging in paper bags (gripped tightly by their owners), everyone settled down to contented sucking or chewing as they resumed the march.

The next section was easy, comprising as it did the steep descent into Roughlee followed by the gentle incline and level road towards Barley. This wasn't as adventurous as the previous stretch because it involved walking on tarmac and passing occasional houses, but was made more pleasurable by the sight ahead of them. The road they followed was now bisecting a stretch of woodland.

Over this darker environment loomed the much closer and more towering bulk of Pendle itself. One had to gaze positively upward in order to clear this great presence and encounter the much brighter cloud-studded sky. The hill was dark, a deep heather and gritstone dark that not even the summer sun could enlighten, though it shone directly on its southern face. The boys gazed in awe at the view which lay before them and which they had to surmount.

Barley village was next with its giggling stream, café, bus stop, village pub and post office. The post office was the target, not that its shop was a scheduled destination but because alongside it ran the public footpath which led once more into open countryside and ever closer to their destination.

Once more the boys strode out with a will, even if calf muscles were beginning to complain. The pathway led the group through meadows, skirting ditches lined with hawthorn bushes, over stone walls via wooden stiles or climbing stones set into the sides. Now and again a desultory ewe would look up from her cropping and gaze at the straggly file until satisfied that they posed no threat.

The trek took the boys steadily upwards until even the cottages of Barley shrank to toy size. Now they were in rough moorland abutting the very foot of Pendle. Despite the height, they still had to tread carefully to avoid the squelchier sections that ran across their path and which it became impossible to entirely avoid. These were the reeds fringed peat bog outcrops which sprang up wherever the soil depth allowed. Elsewhere there were outcrops of hard gritstone which provided fleeting moments of firmer footing. This was serious exploration country.

It was Trevor who broke the spell of careful ground searching by declaring, "Look! The path to the top starts just over there!"

This observation was followed by another rush of whirling arms and legs as they each tried to secure the honour of first foot on the mountain climb. This merely resulted in an untidy tumble of bodies as they converged on the spot. Laughing and jostling one another until they collapsed into a muddied heap, the gang paused to draw breath and rearrange kitbags.

"Now," declared Brian of the authoritative mien, "we need to go in single file or we'll spoil the pathway by wearing away the edge."

The group could see the logic in this, especially as Jimmy had tried to worm his way past Brian and had managed to dislodge a couple of small stones.

"See, what did I tell you!" was the reward he got for his efforts.

Now the real climb began. So steep was the walk now that forward progress was only possible by lifting the leading foot as if climbing stairs. Soon the boys resorted to pushing down with their hands on each thigh as it reached out in order to lever themselves up. After about two hundred or so such ache-inducing moves, they were forced to collapse into the heather, which was now the dominant vegetation. Digging in their heels in order to avoid sliding back down the slope, they leaned back to survey their progress and the splendid view which they had already attained. There below them was the Ogden Reservoir like a pewter mirror set deep in the cleft of the fields. Individual sheep, as well as cattle lower down, could of course still be seen, but they were mere dots in the landscape.

To Tommy's great surprise there were much closer inhabitants on the very slopes upon which they rested. He discovered this as he heard the bleat of a mother sheep calling to its lamb at about the same time as his hand made contact with a little pile of droppings by his side. Luckily they were old droppings and were quite dry. Nevertheless he was obliged to wipe his hand down Robert's back to remove some of the sticky stuff. Robert, of course, didn't take kindly to this and pursued Tommy through the heather until they both fell over and rolled several yards downhill. Extricating themselves, they laboured back up to rejoin the group, which by now had risen to collective feet to resume the climb. More hundreds of short, muscle-aching steps relieved by two more stops were made.

It was Ronnie who halted the exhilarated but now tiring group with a cry of, "The top's just up here!" as he pointed skywards. Almost as one, the boys collapsed gratefully onto the heather at the side of the upwardly angling path. Of course, they were only being polite by waiting for the pair of stragglers to catch up. These in turn excused their tardiness by claiming that they were admiring the view, not struggling to keep up. True enough, it was a grand sight to see the distant roofs and chimneys of the Colne-Burnley conurbation from their lofty viewing point. To think that they had walked all the way from down there in less than three hours!

"OK lads! [Brian of course.] Let's go straight up from here – last one's a monkey."

Cue much puffing, straining of calf muscles and grabbing of heather clumps as they each hauled themselves manfully up the last fifty feet or so until finally they all stood proudly on the summit. Well, not quite, for there was some higher ground off to the left. However, they were perched on the "big end" looking over to Colne and beyond it Yorkshire.

Now they each sought some reasonably dry ground on which to perch while they rummaged in their packs for their well-earned provisions. With an orchestrated unscrewing of tops, they lifted bottles to parched lips and breathlessly swallowed gulps of their chosen nectar between intakes of air and some near hysterical giggling.

Thirst having been assuaged, they set about hungrily attacking lunch. There were jam, cheese, meat, banana and goodness knows what fillings – not all of them finding the mouth of the owner as there was some serious bartering of provisions. Did an apple equal a cheese sandwich? Was a jam butty a fair swap for a small slice of apple pie? No matter, they each concentrated on emptying their lunch packs to lessen the weight on the return journey. No one even considered leaving any litter on the hallowed ground. When Jimmy's paper bag blew away he was told in no uncertain terms to make sure that he retrieved it before it was lost to the elements.

Lunch was just about finished when Ronnie produced his *piece de resistance*. The group watched in open-mouthed fascination as he proceeded to break into a can of *mandarin oranges*! With a flourish he produced a teaspoon and set about extracting the juicy segments as if it were the most normal thing to do on a picnic. Once they got over their shock, the boys began to beseech him for a sliver of orange or a spoonful of the syrupy juice. Their entreaties had no effect whatsoever. With some justification, albeit tempered with a certain smugness, he reminded them, "You've eaten your stuff and didn't offer me any for nothing!"

"Yeah, but we would have done if we knew you had mandarin oranges," countered Robert.

"I've never had them," said Jimmy rather wistfully.

"No? Well, you're not getting any now either," replied Ronnie, and this seemed to end the discussion apart from the odd jealous muttering and some dirty looks aimed in his direction. It was generally accepted that only Ronnie's posh mum would think of providing such fare on an adventure day out.

After the lunchtime clearing up, the party hiked across to the dry stone wall and the stepping stones set into its side. Tommy wondered about the necessity of constructing such a boundary on the very summit of this virtual mountain…

One by one they clambered over the divide and regathered in the tussocky field which marked the termination of the "big end" of Pendle. Here was to be found a most magnificent view. When the boys had wiped clear their eyes, which had become wet with tears by dint of the stiffness of the breeze, they gazed upon the panorama of the West Craven district of Yorkshire. Spread before them were rounded hilltops and meadows, criss-crossed by the ubiquitous stone walls that reeled their way drunkenly around the contours of the fields. Little matchbox farm buildings could be made out now and then. There in the distance was Blacko Tower, poking up like a chimney from the roof of a rounded hillock but still far beneath the lofty splendour of Pendle.

As their eyes took in the vast sweep of open country that lay before them, Brian seized the opportunity to state that, "You can see five counties from up here!"

The group were at a loss to comprehend this statistic, so they began to reel off the possibilities. Certainly Lancashire and Yorkshire were on the list (obviously), but where next? Could that be a bit of Derbyshire far to the south? What about Westmoreland to the north-west? If Derbyshire could be seen, then how about Cheshire next door? Whatever the truth, it was certainly impressed upon the boys that Pendle was indeed a most lofty perch and perhaps worthy of being called a mountain. If that was the case, it was the only mountain that any of them could lay claim to having scaled.

When the group had managed to use up most of their surplus energy, having slogged around the summit on one caper or another, it was time to consider a return to home ground. Packs were made secure, arms and legs brushed clear of grass and heather and socks pulled up tight. The descent of the steep path proved almost as demanding as the climb, for it meant uneven leaps and leg-jarring braking manoeuvres in order to avoid tumbling down the vertiginous hillside.

Eventually they made it without undue mishap and gratefully eased their straining calf muscles onto the more level and much springier turf of the rough pastures. Barley village was reached, tramped through and left behind as they headed towards Roughlee. Once more, a steep ascent up the narrow lane led them back to the oasis of Noggarth Top. Those happy few who still had a little money quickly parted with it in exchange for chewy sweets and iced lollies.

Thus it was well into teatime when the tired but happy band split up on arrival at Beaufort Street, each member to retire to a grateful hearth and a welcoming meal.

Rainy Days and Bonfires

I nevitably, not all of the summer was as balmy as the last days had been. In fact, there were many times when Tommy had to resort to his button collection to pass away the dreariest of rain-soaked afternoons, which precluded even the most hardy from gathering for outside play.

From the large glass jar tumbled a substantial collection of buttons, marbles, ball-bearings, tiddlywinks, dice and all manner of items as Tommy upended it on the lounge carpet. Now, what will it be today – football or war games? The latter choice won the day. Tommy set about the task of selecting buttons which could be roughly grouped into two sets according to colour. The black and grey ones would comprise one army and the other colours the enemy force. So, what famous event would be re-enacted on the carpet on this fitful afternoon – The World War (first or second), Napoleon versus Wellington, the American Civil War, Roman legions repelling the Hun or US cavalry against the Plains Indians? All of these titanic clashes were embedded in Tommy's memory, owing more to his avid digestion of comic strips and library books than any benefit accruing from formal education.

The opposing factions were duly and meticulously arranged in contrasting formations on the carpet. One side comprised rigid, box-like regiments and the other a ragged assortment of marauders – clansmen or savages obviously. The battle commenced as soon as a die was thrown. If the number revealed was 1, 2 or 3, a success was attributed to one army and a 4, 5 or 6 gave credit to the enemy. Each throw of the dice removed one button (soldier) from the losing side.

Between throws the formations were adjusted so that the opposing forces drew ever closer together. Eventually, this resulted in hand-to-hand combat with a continuous shaking of the die until all of one side were vanquished. In this manner Tommy was able to pass away an otherwise dreary afternoon in rewarding fashion.

If a full-scale war failed to excite, there remained the option of a football match with button players and pearl bead ball. Either of these games was, of course, only indulged in private by Tommy alone. Even his best mate Robert wouldn't have appreciated such imaginative play.

But there was a limit to the number of Cup Finals and epic battles that even Tommy could endure before frustration and enforced lassitude got the better of him. At such times he would don raincoat and sturdy shoes and venture forth even in the most miserable of drizzly days. Down to the town centre he would trudge, there to gaze once more into the windows of the toy model shop, the sweet shops and even the Co-op with its varied display. The chemist window held brief fascination before Tommy headed for his inevitable sanctuary – the local library. At least there he could pass some time in peace and warmth.

It never failed to stimulate Tommy's senses each time he pushed open the large wooden door with the brass handle which admitted him to the children's section of the library. Reassuringly, there was the children's head librarian herself perched behind her well worn and polished desk. Miss Mann seldom greeted any child with anything more than the hint of a smile, but this was sufficient encouragement for Tommy.

He headed for the non-fiction shelves to see if there was any exciting volume that might capture his attention. After browsing through a book on African exploration he turned instead to his favourite shelf in the fiction section – that containing the works of Richmal Crompton. Sure enough, there were several volumes of the *Just William* books.

Now William was a particular hero of Tommy's, not least because of his rebellious streak and the fact that he got away with murder in dealings with his family, especially with his older sister with whom he enjoyed a love–hate relationship. This struck a particular chord with Tommy, though he could never imagine having the nerve to get into the scrapes that William endured.

Anyway, William usually got his comeuppance at some point, even if this was just a tweaked ear or a vigorous scrubbing from the housemaid. How did such a scruffy and unruly boy have a lifestyle that involved cooks and house-maids? Perhaps that was part of the mystique of the enigma that was William.

A sudden outburst of giggling from the far side of the room interrupted these musings. Tommy's head shot up and he stared across at the source of this rude intrusion, but it subsided almost immediately upon a withering glare from Miss Mann directed at the two contrite girls who were the cause of the commotion. They had seemingly found something highly amusing in an illustrated book from the science section.

Tommy recognised one of them as a school acquaintance of his (not that he would admit knowing Stephanie Duffy – the silly twit). He derived a certain satisfaction from watching her having to bite her lower lip in order to stem another fit of the giggles that would surely have resulted in the two being ejected from the premises.

Not wishing to be associated with such immature behaviour, Tommy quickly chose two *William* titles (one of which he had already read) and made his way to Miss Mann's desk. He was pleasantly surprised when she not only spoke to him but also imparted some welcome news.

"You are allowed to take out three books now if you wish," she beamed down at him.

"Oh, thanks," breathed Tommy as if she was conferring some special privilege on him alone. "I'll just go and get another one."

So saying, he scooted quietly back to the non-fiction section, carefully avoiding eye contact with the silly girls, and picked out a book on jungle exploration that had attracted his attention before.

When he emerged into daylight, Tommy was delighted to discover that the dreary drizzle had passed and the sun was trying to break out from the clutches of the banks of cloud. Vapour was beginning to rise from the pavement flags and the air felt fresher and warmer on his face. With spirit uplifted, Tommy set off at a brisk pace for home.

Once in his room, he set about the first of his story books – the one he had not previously read. He had reached chapter five before Mum called him down to tea.

After tea there was even time and daylight left for a game of cricket on the back street. Several of the lads had come together for a limited-overs match in which each member of the team bowled six balls at the opposing side. After the allotted four overs from Tommy's team, the other side had scored twenty-eight runs. This total included a four when the ball passed the end of the street, and a "four and out" when one batsman hit a delivery over a backyard gate. Three of the opposition had got themselves out in this innings.

Tommy's team only managed twenty-five in reply, but then again Jimmy on the opposing side had cheated because he kept bowling the ball into a dip where a cobblestone had sunk and thus the ball continually reared up at all sorts of crazy and unplayable angles.

All argument about the fairness of the situation subsided when everyone agreed that they would have all done the same thing if only they had thought of it first. The games session concluded with a bout of ball tig, in which the tennis ball used in the match became a missile hurled at the legs of everyone fleeing from the one who was "on". Truce was only called when a combination of approaching dusk and the demanding calls of mothers and older sisters summoned each of the boys to their respective homes.

So it was that summer passed into autumn. The days, or more pertinently the evening playing-out time, grew ever shorter. The air, despite the dryness of the weather, grew progressively cooler until the smell of the bonfire season pervaded the senses. Bonfire night itself may only last one evening, but it required weeks of preparation: there was the ceaseless quest to find suitable material to burn; a site on which to construct the pyre; guard duty to be arranged and not least, funds to be raised to provide for a fitting pyro-technic display.

It was generally accepted that one didn't attempt to secure funding from one's parents, who would only have insisted on exercising a degree of control with regard to the purchasing of the fireworks (thus resulting in a safe but boring collection). The exception was of course Ronnie, whose mum would not hear of him having anything but the best of the lot and therefore bestowed ample funds on him.

The other lads were quite content to be financially inde-pendent and rely on their own initiative to raise the required funds.

So, on several October evenings when the weather allowed, which was any time when it wasn't pouring down, the boys, along with any girls who were accepted, took to the local streets. More precisely, they toured the backstreets as they knew that they wouldn't be tolerated knocking on anyone's front door.

In groups of two or three they set out to cover the neighbourhood. The prescribed method was to visit every house on one side of the backstreet and come back on the other side, thus covering every household. The first move involved one of the group clicking open the latch on the backyard gate. If this wasn't bolted (there were a few unsociable folk) the gate would be slowly opened. Great care was taken at this stage lest there should be a fierce hound lying in wait. If the coast was clear the group would shuffle across the yard and assemble by the rear window and door. It always lifted their spirits if there was a light showing in the back room, where most families spent their evenings.

There was one such promising beacon shining from the rear window of Number 5 Extwistle Street as the two boys carefully lifted the latch of the backyard gate and crept towards the door. It was Robert's shrill voice which first pierced the evening gloom, shortly followed by that of Tommy as he attempted to keep in step, if not in tune, as they chorused together:

> "Remember, remember, the fifth of November,
> It's Gunpowder Plot – we never forgot.
> Put your hand in your pocket
> and pull out your purse,
> a ha'penny or a penny will do you no worse."

In case the family within had not heard this cacophony, Robert followed up with:

> "Knock at the door, ring at the bell,
> See what you get for singing so well!"

One thing the boys could not be accused of was underestimating their talents. At least that was the conclusion they came to as the lady of the house pressed a threepenny bit into Tommy's palm with a whispered, "Thank you."

It never occurred to either of them that perhaps the occupants were glad to be rid of such entertainment or, in the case of Tommy who was a Catholic, that it was something of an irony that he should be singing in celebratory fashion the demise of one of his faith forefathers.

As they left the yard they could hear the distant tones of:

"Bonfire night, the stars shine bright…"

This particular rendition ended with a sharp tattoo on the rear door by the perpetrators followed by:

"…please put a penny in the old man's hat.
If you haven't got a penny a ha'penny will do,
if you haven't got a ha'penny then god bless you."

Although what their pals would have thought of any householder who professed themselves to be too poor to spare a copper or two didn't bear thinking about. Any contribution was deemed acceptable, even a ha'penny, especially if the occupants were really old (which meant pensionable age to the boys).

Experience told that the welcome could and often did vary from a hostile *"clear off"* (thankfully not too frequent) through *"someone's already been"*, which was fair enough, to a rewarding response. This was usually in the form of copper coinage – a mixture of farthings, halfpennies, pennies and tuppences. Just occasionally, as in Robert and Tommy's case, there might be a brass threepenny bit or even, if rarely, a little silver sixpence.

A good evening might bring a harvest of two shillings or so to be divided between three boys – ample funds to buy several fireworks each, ranging from penny bangers to tuppenny or thruppenny snowy cascades, roman candles or vesuviuses.

The two separate groups of troubadours met at the junction of Extwistle Street and Bradshaw Street to compare pickings. Billy, Wendy and Eric had amassed one shilling and nine pence, which just beat Robert and Tommy's haul by a penny-ha'penny. However, the latter group's haul only had to be split two ways, which meant that they each got ninepence ha'penny and tossed for the other ha'penny, which Robert won.

Two more evenings of singing around the neighbouring backstreets, one of which took place on a foggy and drizzly night, meant that by the time bonfire night arrived the boys had more than half a crown each. This was supplemented in Tommy's case by another two shillings from his dad.

This made possible the purchase of a whole range of pyrotechnic delights, including penny bangers, penny ha'penny jumping jacks, two penny catherine wheels and thrupenny rockets and roman candles. The only items they had difficulty purchasing were the bangers as old Atkins wouldn't sell them to unaccompanied children.

The bonfire itself was a splendid sight on the night of the fifth of November. It had been painstakingly constructed on the spare land between the bungalows on Causey Foot and the allotments. It was stacked high with an assortment of discarded planks and sheets of plywood, palettes, old furniture and lots of brushwood and branches which seemed to have become detached from their natural growing places. There was also a generous pile of replacement kindling for topping up the conflagration.

The evening's weather produced a classical breezy and damp atmosphere, though it wasn't actually raining. The coats that everyone wore were more for protection from the incendiary devices than any threat from the clouds.

Several dads soon got the fire lit with the help of a good dowsing of paraffin liberally sprinkled over the woodwork. Eagerly the flames licked at the jumble of lumber until a roaring blaze was achieved. With the assistance of the wind, this soon gave rise to a swirling cloud of smoke and sparks that caused eyes to water and, in not a few instances, grit to sting the eyeballs.

There was some attempt by the adults in self-appointed charge to organise the fireworks properly. Rockets had to be handed over in order to be inserted into the tops of milk bottles which were part buried in the earth. Other fireworks promising glittering and cascading displays were set off one at a time on the low brick wall which housed a drainage pipe.

Each burst of colour and sparks was greeted with a chorus of "ooh"s and "aah"s and the occasional clapping of hands or raucous laughter from the older spectators.

Still there were opportunities for the more mischievous boys to light jumping jacks behind the girls and watch them scream and dance like demented puppets in order to avoid being scorched. Quite a few youngsters were quite content to hold sparklers and trace glowing patterns in the air with them, though Robert and Tommy would never be seen doing this in company.

As the bonfire heap began to collapse and take on a much hotter and brighter glow, large potatoes were gingerly placed near the outer edges and poked towards the embers with large sticks whilst the erstwhile cooks shielded their faces from the fierce heat.

Mrs Edmondson, the wife of the baker whose shop was across the road from Atkin's sweet shop, flourished a large paper bag of home-made "plot toffee" and almost unnecessarily announced, "Anyone want a piece of treacle?"

She was almost submerged by a swarm of eager hands and cries of, "Me!", "Me... me... me!" and even "Me, please, Mrs Edmonson!". Beaming with pleasure at the delighted reception her confectionery had induced, Mrs E produced another bagful and passed it among the adults until many mouths were full. With bulging cheeks and lips oozing melted treacle, there was much contented sucking and chewing among children and grown-ups alike.

The families with smaller children finally began to drift homeward long past their offsprings' bedtimes. This gave more opportunity for the older lads and the more intrepid girls to play with the much smaller, though still fiercely hot bonfire. They poked around in the hope of finding a last scorched potato, though the ones already consumed had consisted of over burnt skins and dubious insides. Flaming brands were brandished and a last few fireworks materialised. These included bangers which had been frowned upon by the more responsible parents.

Amazingly, no one received any serious damage or burn despite this wanton cavorting – that is unless Brian's ripped pocket or Greta's scratched leg (caused by a protruding nail in a piece of firewood) counted as injuries.

At last the remaining diehards drifted off home with blackened faces and their clothes reeking of smoke, no doubt to receive the collective wrath of their maternal elders.

Christmas

Halloween, with its apple bobbing and scary tales, was but a distant memory. Now the delights of bonfire night too had faded into the misty recesses of an increasingly chilly winter. There were occasional bitterly cold days when the weather came over the Pennines from the east. Days when fingers were numbed and bones jarred from ice-induced slides and tumbles onto the unforgiving cobbles and stone flags. Days when the few cars in the neighbourhood, along with the buses and vans, slithered and skewed across the roads and had to be pushed through drifting snow. Days when coal fires were banked up to ward off the invasion of frost into kitchens and bedrooms.

Now at least there was the promise of Christmas. Most of the provisions for the feast had been gathered by the Calvert family. This included jars of home-made pickles, biscuit tins stacked with Mrs C's mince pies – heavily laced with brandy and Dad's supply of lager. It was time to collect the tree itself.

Tommy had for several days watched with increasing envy the parlours of other households whose windows were illuminated by the twinkling coloured lights festooning trees of all sizes. Some were artificial trees, but no matter; they still looked magical when complete with tinsel, lametta and baubles all reflecting the rainbows of coloured bulbs.

Only a real tree would suffice in the Calvert household, so Tommy was eager and ready when his mum announced, "Get your coat on, lad, and come and help me bring home the tree."

The two of them set out pursued by cries of, "Get a nice big one!", "Make sure it's a good shape!" and, "We don't want one that'll lose its needles before Christmas Day!" As if they needed telling about careful choosing with all their experience of making quality purchases!

It was a good three-quarters of a mile to the yard of the Corporation Waterworks, but Mrs Calvert knew that this was the place for the best choice and price. There was a light dusting of snow on the ground when they reached the yard but this only lent enchantment to the scene. There were dozens of pines and firs stacked drunkenly in the compound. Mrs Calvert circled them with beady eye, stood several upright and made Tommy hold them while she scrutinised each for healthiness, spread of branches and height.

Eventually one came nearer than the rest to satisfying her requirements (including price), though Tommy wasn't convinced it would be large enough. He was made to revise this opinion as they struggled home, Mum holding the base of the trunk and Tommy endeavouring to keep a grip on the top, whilst being pricked by the needles and having the uppermost branches poking him in various parts of his head.

When they reached home they were obliged to lean the tree against the back yard wall until Dad had time to fashion a base from a bucket, some sand and assorted pieces of wood. Meanwhile, Shirley served a grateful Mum with a reviving glass of cream sherry. Tommy had had to help himself to a glass of Bulmer's cider from the Christmas stock.

It was now just a week and a half to Christmas day. Mr Calvert, with hints from his wife, had deemed that this was close enough to put up the decorations. Out from the attic store came the cardboard box holding the items from previous Christmases. These included various crepe paper designs as well as the glass baubles for the tree and the tangle of wire and bulbs that would light up the tree.

This year the ageing collection had been updated and supplemented by some new purchases thriftily hoarded by Mrs Calvert out of her wages. There were balloons, crackers and some chocolate and plastic novelties to fill up the branches.

"Who wants to help with the streamers?" announced Dad.

"I will," chorused Shirley and Tommy virtually simultaneously.

With a rare display of cooperation, the two children took a long length of red and one of green crepe paper. They retired to opposite ends of the living room and proceeded to twist their ends of paper in opposite directions. The result was a quite striking streamer of red and green with fairly evenly sized twists. They carefully passed the ends one at a time to Dad, who was perched atop a step ladder. He tacked the ends to the ceiling using drawing pins. Soon the room was filled with different coloured bunting radiating from the light shade in the centre of the room to the corners and side walls – eight streamers in total. The ends were further embellished with little clusters of balloons.

It was only after Tommy and Shirley's faces had turned a bright purple with the strain of inflating each balloon with lung power alone that Mum suddenly remembered, "Oh, heck! I've got one of those inflating cylinders that I bought on the market the week before last!"

At least dad seemed to find it funny, so much so that he nearly fell off his perch when he burst out laughing at their expressions.

When they had recovered sufficiently, they set to the task of shaping the three-dimensional decorations. These were bells, hemispheres and crackers made of crepe paper with cardboard strengtheners and which were folded flat. They had to be opened out and fastened with little clips to hold them in position. These too were set along the walls.

Eventually it was the turn of the tree. First it was draped with the lights. Only two of them didn't light up when tested, but these soon worked when the bulbs were tightened up. The cat had already begun to scatter the lametta and roll away a few of the baubles before they could be fastened on the tree. This was an art in itself to cover the wires and distribute the ornaments equally. The only trouble was there were several artists at work at once. The result was not entirely symmetrical but the effect of elaborate over adornment was achieved.

Mrs Calvert insisted on an immediate switch-on to gain the full effect of their toil. She was sufficiently impressed to break open one of the two bottles of home-made festive advocaat and to pour everyone a sherry-sized measure. Tommy was included in the round, even though the mixture was liberally laced with brandy which gave it quite a kick as well as a most delicious flavour far removed from commercial brands.

What with the previously downed cider and this on top, Tommy was obliged to retire in order to sleep off the effects.

Christmas Eve arrived. Meals were quite frugal and plain by tradition, in contrast to the excesses that the following day would bring. The family clustered around the fire and listened intently to the radio, which produced a mixture of comedy and solemnity with sprinklings of hymns and yuletide music. This was only interrupted when one of Dad's workmates called round with his family to exchange festive greetings. Out came the sherry and lager, the latter to be mixed with lime for the ladies. Even Tommy was allowed a small glass of this. Shirley stuck to tomato juice sprinkled with Worcester sauce.

After the friends had departed, it was time to get ready for the walk down to St Joseph's Church for Midnight Mass. Tommy was quite bog-eyed by now but had no intentions of missing the chance to stay awake past the magical hour. Besides, he couldn't really be left alone in the house.

He, along with the rest of the family, soon woke up when they left the glowing fireplace and stepped outside. It hadn't snowed but instead it was a crisp and clear cloudless night and the stars sparkled like diamonds until everyone's eyes watered and dimmed the spectacle. Collars and buttons were done up and they set out gingerly, mindful of the sheen of frost on the flagstones. Their breath rose and drifted on the still night air as they laughed and chattered their way down the streets and across the main road. By now there were several other groups making their way to the same destination. Some had come not from home but directly from pubs and clubs, a fact that would later become plain to Tommy as he sat among them in the pews and detected the reek of alcohol on their breath.

Mum regarded this as some form of blasphemy, to participate in the Mass when far from sober. However, the church was full to bursting just after half eleven. As the time for Mass approached, there was not a seat in the house. Several dozen of the congregation were obliged to line the side aisles and back wall of the nave, there to spend the entire Mass standing up. These unfortunates were mostly the ones who had unwisely stayed for one last drink before setting off. A kind of justice there, thought Mum.

The organist was in full flow and the gathering sang the usual carols with great gusto. The advent of the priest was preceded by the senior altar server, a grown-up, who emerged to light the myriad candles on the altar and sanctuary. Then came two pairs of bleary eyed younger altar servers leading the procession for the start of Mass.

As far as Tommy was concerned, the whole ceremony passed in a blur of noise, flickering light and shuffling responses. More than once he had had to knuckle his weary eyeballs in order to maintain a semblance of awareness. At last it was over. The families crowding out jostled their way down the exit steps like a football crowd leaving the scene of play. Out onto Macleod Street they tumbled. Instantly the freezing night air revived many and sobered a few until they recovered sufficiently to swap festive greetings and embraces.

"Merry Christmas!" was heard to pierce the night-time air several times in Tommy's vicinity, along with, "All the best!", God bless now", "And you too!" Tommy merely grinned self-consciously and waved when he spied Stella with her brother and the rest of her family.

It wasn't long before each group turned and headed for the sanctuary of their homes where cheery lights and refreshments awaited. By the time the Calverts reached their own front door Tommy was just about all in. Shedding their boots, coats and scarves they trudged through the hallway and into the living room where they were met with a blast of heat from the still glowing coal fire.

Dad made a bee-line for the sherry bottle and poured out generous measures for himself and Mum. Tommy and Shirley helped themselves to glasses of fizzy and cloudy lemonade. The gramophone player was switched on in order to blare out the voice of Harry Belafonte singing about the joy of the Nativity.

A grateful Tommy was soon packed off to bed in order to be asleep for Santa's visit. Did he still believe in him? He wasn't at all sure, but now was not the time to have doubts with the promise of waking up to some lovely surprise…

"Are you awake yet, lad?" completed the climb back from slumber to consciousness.

Gosh, was it morning already? Tommy tumbled out of bed and hurried to the bathroom before scurrying down the stairs two at a time and half dressed. Mum and Dad were already there with cups of tea and thick buttered toast.

"Well, aren't you going to open it?" urged Dad, nodding in the direction of a huge parcel lying in front of the tree.

Needing no further invitation, Tommy snatched it up and quickly tore away the layers of wrapping paper to reveal the large cardboard box emblazoned with the magic title "Hornby Dublo" and a picture of a wonderful steam train racing across the countryside.

The only uttering he could make was a gasping, *"Wow!"* as he carefully lifted the lid. He caressed the bright green livery of the locomotive before reverently lifting it out of its cradle. He turned it round, noting first the nameplate "Duchess of Montrose" then the pistons and wheels and the driver's box. After a few excited minutes examining the rest of the set, the trackwork was put together and connected up to the mains via the transformer.

Tommy set the switch and turned the dial until the magnificent train was winding its way around the oval track. Even Mum stopped her preparations in the kitchen to watch along with the rest of the proud and impressed family.

Eventually they all retired to the fireplace and the tree for the unveiling of the rest of the family's gifts to one another. These were, to Tommy's eyes, the boring collection of toiletries, clothing, confectionery and gadgets that passed for presents with the adults and Shirley. He had to admit to being well pleased with his own growing mound of books and toys, though he would have been quite satisfied just with the train set, to which he returned while the others passed their treasures round for inspection.

Some time later, Mum bustled in with a plate of bacon (the rinds carefully cut off and fried separately as crisps) and thick slices of bread. This was merely a snack to break their fast as a prelude to dinner itself, though how Mum found the time to do this as well as roasting the turkey and preparing the veg was a source of wonderment.

The radio was switched on for the Christmas messages

and music, though Tommy was engrossed in the music of the engine wheels whirring round the track. Dad was dispensing largesse and liquid refreshment – lager and lime, brown ale and ginger beer.

Dinner, when it arrived, was a feast that covered the whole dining table fully extended. There was scarcely room for the crackers to be placed above each setting, between the prawn cocktail dishes and the pudding spoons. There was the turkey in prime position, along with bowls of roast potatoes, sprouts, carrots and peas. There were the gravy, stuffing and bread sauce containers to be accommodated. Soon there was a clinking and jangling of utensils before a contented silence descended as each attacked their over-crowded platefuls with a relish and a will.

"Hold on a moment everybody," interrupted Dad, as he stilled the action to make a toast. "A very Happy Christmas to everyone, and thanks to Ma for this wonderful dinner!"

There was a ritual clinking of glasses and muttered replies before they all resumed the attack on their laden portions.

"Who's for pudding?" called out Mum unnecessarily some time later. They were all stuffed but no one was going to pass up the chance to tuck into rich fruit pudding with brandy sauce. The mince pies would have to wait till digestion allowed room for them as well.

At last they all staggered to reclining positions on the sofa and chairs in order to help down their food with more drink.

Some soporific hours later, less for Mum and Dad who had to clear and wash the dishes, the evening descended into chatter, word games and a nut-cracking and sweet eating marathon until everyone was ready to call it a night in order to be able to be ready for Boxing Day. This would involve more bingeing, visits from friends and a walk into the nearby country lanes to clear heads and stomachs.

Winter

There was no snow to speak of for the rest of Christmas. For this Mr Calvert at least was grateful. It meant that the family could visit his wife's mother and sister, a journey which meant a drive of some one and a half hours to reach Liverpool and the district of Kirkdale where they lived. Tommy and Shirley passed the time on the trip through Burnley, Whalley and Preston counting and comparing the Christmas trees they could spot in the front room windows as they passed through the residential districts.

Maghull was the first part of what they considered to be Merseyside rather than merely part of Lancashire. It was New Year's Eve, although still afternoon, when they pulled into Juliet Street and drew up outside the cosy terraced house where Nanna and Aunt Marie lived.

Tommy was first to the door and he enthusiastically drummed on the knocker to announce their arrival. Marie answered and beamed with delight on seeing her relatives, who came all too infrequently. Soon it was hugs and kisses all round (mercifully Tommy was spared most of these) as they were ushered into the back living room.

"How are yer? Lovely to see you," grinned Nanna Hannah. "Come on in and sit yourselves down now. Marie'll put the kettle on and make youse a nice cup of tea."

"Now don't be making a fuss," replied Mrs Calvert, somewhat in vain, for she knew that that was exactly what they would do.

"Tommy lad, will you do me a favour?" called Auntie Marie from the kitchen. Tommy was up in a flash for he knew it wouldn't be anything taxing or his auntie wouldn't ask. It seemed that she wanted him to go and get a packet of biscuits from the shop on Stanley Road, just round the corner from the top of the street.

"Seeing as you're going will you get Nanna some of her snuff as well, and here's an extra tuppence to get yourself some sweeties."

"You shouldn't spoil him, Marie," argued Mrs C, equally wastefully.

Tommy didn't think he was going to spoil for the sake of a few sweets, and anyway, he knew that his auntie loved to treat him. Off he raced to the end of the street. Once on the main road he paused briefly to gaze at the stream of traffic heading into and out of the city. He loved to see the buses in their red livery, such a contrast to the drab cream and maroon ones in Nelson.

He pushed open the door of Martha's sweet, tobacco and general goods shop and inhaled the special aroma it contained, again unlike anything experienced at home.

"Penn'orth of snuff please, Martha," he intoned to the pleasant old lady behind the counter.

"Hello, young one. Visiting your grandma again, are you?" she replied while attending to his order. This she did by dipping a scoop into a sweet-type jar. She skilfully withdrew the correct quantity of snuff and poured it carefully into a small white paper bag. She completed the process by twisting the bag tightly closed and handing it over along with the liquorice confection that Tommy had pointed out. While this was going on, Tommy's gaze roved along the shelves, taking in the dozens of jars and tins which lined the walls. There was everything that a family might need to hand – soap, matches, tinned food, firelighters, bottles of cordial and fizzy drink, washing line, shoe polish and all manner of cleaning items. All this as well as a good selection of sweets and cigarettes.

Clutching the biscuits, snuff and sweets, Tommy turned to the exit.

"Go careful now!" Martha cried to his back as he swung out of the door.

When he had made it halfway down Juliet Street, Tommy met a young boy and girl he had seen on a previous visit.

"Are yer comin' out to play?" enquired the lad.

"All right then," said Tommy, "but first I have to take this in to my nanna."

Mission accomplished, Tommy was allowed to go back out onto the street, "Only for a short time, mind."

The two children he had met were now sitting on a garden wall several doors along. Tommy walked across, felt the wall to see how cold it was and noted that, unlike the stone walls of his home streets, the brick ones in Liverpool would not offer a serious challenge to his bare legs.

He hunched up alongside the boy, who turned out to be called Jimmy. On Jimmy's other side sat Betty, his sister, who gave Tommy a searching gaze.

"Where'd you come from then?" she directed at him.

"Nelson."

"Where's that? I've never heard of it." Jimmy this time.

Tommy endeavoured to explain that it was miles away at the other side of Lancashire but he could tell that this didn't really enlighten them any further.

"What's yer name, anyway?" interrupted Betty again.

After acquaintances had been established, Jimmy offered to take Tommy on a local tour by way of walking along the garden walls and leaping across the gaps between each house front (no one had a gate). Betty followed in equally agile fashion, though Tommy noted that they didn't attempt to walk along the wall of Number 5, from the front window of which glared the visage of a spindly and pinched woman with a face like wrinkled wax.

Jimmy explained that his dad was a docker. As such, he and his sister occasionally had treats. These included toffee made using sugar that his dad had managed to bring home after a day's work unloading the cargo boats.

At the end of the street, Jimmy endeavoured to lead the party along Oriel Road and on to Macbeth Street. Tommy declined. His explanation that he was under strict orders to return to Nanna's house imminently was accepted by the pair, especially when Tommy donated one of his liquorice sticks to them to be shared.

Pushing open the front door of Number 24, Tommy entered the lobby. He glanced to his left to peer into the parlour, though he knew no one would be in there. It was a well-kept though seldom used room. The thick drapes and faded lace curtains allowed enough light to fall on the tiled fireplace and the cocktail cabinet that occupied the far wall. The only other notable item of furniture in the room was a bed settee which would no doubt be occupied by his nanna and auntie tonight when Mum and Dad were given the use of the front bedroom.

Everyone was settled in the living room enjoying tea and biscuits when Tommy entered. Aunt Marie immediately got up to fuss over Tommy, fetching him a drink of squash and some biscuits.

Tommy happily settled on the floor in front of the wonderful range that always fascinated him. While they had coal fires at home, nothing approached the splendour of his nanna's. Set into the chimney breast, the black metal range had a central raised fire grate. This was flanked by two side ovens. The tops doubled as cooking hobs and flat iron warmers. Tommy knew that as well as giving off a splendid warm glow, the whole construction was too hot to be touched. Access could only be by adults armed either with thick, heat-proof mitts or the peculiar rod used to flick open the oven doors or remove an item from the hob.

Between the range and the small rear window was a built-in wall cupboard with open shelves that housed Nanna's few precious ornaments. These included a toby jug, a statue of a grand lady with a flowing dress, another blue Devon cream jug brought back from holiday by Tommy's mum and the little model cottage that Tommy himself had bought for Nanna. This had been from their Welsh holiday two years before.

"How are you enjoying school then? I bet you're a clever lad now, eh?" enthused Aunt Marie.

Tommy gave a sickly grin and muttered a rather embarrassed reply, especially as he caught a glimpse of Shirley's expression out of the corner of his eye. Just because Auntie hadn't asked her first!

Mum came to the rescue. "He regularly gets good marks for his work and we think he'll do well in the tests this year." The tests being the eleven-plus. Tommy would reach that age next summer and would thus have to undergo the process to decide his school future.

Thankfully the topic of conversation moved on to more pleasant subjects. Tommy's interest in the proceedings was enlivened by the sight of his nanna taking her snuff. Pulling out the paper bag from her large apron, she proceeded to expertly remove a pinch between her thumb and forefinger. Jamming these into each nostril in turn, she inhaled. Soon afterwards she blew into a large coloured handkerchief which became stained with the nicotine. She returned Tommy's gaze and chuckled heartily.

Tommy was sent to the kitchen to wash his hands for tea. First, though, he had to visit the outside toilet, another unique experience. This was at the far end of the small backyard. He lifted the latch and edged into the dark and cold cubicle. He peered down into the bowl, which was a deep structure set in a wooden bench seat. The drain was far below.

As he began to use the toilet he was most alarmed to hear and then spot the figure of a boy of about the same age as himself. He was standing on the top of the wall on the opposite side and making rude and scornful remarks, which Tommy tried his best to ignore. He hurried back inside.

The kitchen sink was a big stone one set into the outside wall. Exposed lead piping ended in a single brass tap which gave cold water. Hot water would come from the kettle simmering on the range. Tommy made do with the tap water and then vigorously dried his hands on the rough, worn towel.

He watched as his auntie pulled down the bureau-type front door of the kitchenette and began to remove plates and cruets. She let Tommy get the cutlery from the drawer and help her to set the dining table, a fold-out affair in the living room. Tea of ham, potatoes and veg was followed by tinned fruit and cream.

It being New Year's Eve, the children were allowed to stay up with the grown-ups. Entertainment was provided by the radio and gramophone, though Tommy's mum, nanna and auntie always found plenty to talk about. Marie even managed to get Dad involved discussing the mixed fortunes of his beloved Liverpool football team, who were languishing in the Second Division. To be truthful, most of their talk was of bygone glory years which were long overdue in returning.

As midnight approached, everyone was caught up in the anticipation of greeting in the New Year. Glasses of sherry were poured ready. Dad was sent out of the back door armed with a lump of coal. His job was to go round the block and knock on the front door. As the chimes of Big Ben sounded on the radio, he was allowed inside as the greeter of the New Year.

Whilst the entire family stood in the lobby and at the door, they could hear the whoops and sirens of the ships in the docks. Sounds of singing made them spill out onto the street.

At the top of the street an amazing sight met their eyes. Large groups of people were forming huge circles in the middle of Stanley Road. With arms linked they were lustily belting out the strains of "Auld Lang Syne" before collapsing into hugging and kissing with backslapping and shouts of "Happy New Year!" Tommy wanted to get closer to this action but, after listening once more to the wails of the distant ships, he was ushered back inside.

It was time for bed. Tommy was to share the front bedroom, using a put-up mattress next to the double bed that his mum and dad would share. His sister Shirley had the single bed in the little back bedroom. He went to bed first but was kept awake for some time listening to the sounds of laughter and drinking from below until he finally nodded off.

On the afternoon of New Year's Day, Aunt Marie took Tommy and Shirley to the matinee film show at the Commodore Cinema just two blocks away on Stanley Road. On the bill was a mix of short films including a Tom Mix Western and a Dean Martin and Jerry Lewis full-length comedy. The children were treated to a carton of orange juice and some sweet popcorn. Tommy's auntie seemed to be enjoying herself as much as he and his sister, and in truth she was making the most of their brief and too infrequent company.

After teatime it was time to be heading for home as Dad had to be at work the following morning and Mum had plenty to get ready before her next shift at the mill. The return journey seemed to be much quicker, though Tommy felt ready for bed soon after they arrived home. He put up a struggle for a while before succumbing to weariness. As he lay in bed thinking back on his visit, he could hear the wind getting up and some gusts of rain or sleet battering the window panes.

The following morning saw the arrival of a fitful and cold spell of wintry weather which descended on the town and kept people indoors apart from the unfortunate ones who had to go to work. Luckily it was still the school holidays.

The local children were delighted when, two days later, it began to snow. It had started in the night and by mid-morning, flurries of lovely large snowflakes begin to drift down on the breeze. This welcome bonus arrived in time for the children to be able to forget the approaching new school term and indulge themselves in some worthwhile winter play.

The first activity was of course snowballing. Each child to emerge from his or her backyard was greeted by their mates with a bombardment of snow grenades. Far from driving them back inside, this encouraged the victims to respond with shrieks of glee as they returned fire.

The snow was nice and thick, soft and fluffy and easy to shape into fist-sized balls which were hurled inaccurately to splatter against walls or occasionally on human targets. Necks soon became sodden with melting and dripping snow, which had to be blown away from eyebrows by upturned lips. Jumpers, pants and socks were adorned with clinging patches of flakes. Faces turned bright red, burnt by the snow but also through the gasping and panting of breathless abandon.

After a truce in order to allow themselves to recover, a few souls dived back to their houses. This was only an interval so that they could find woollen gloves and dry scarves to tuck into saturated collars. It was time to bring out the sledges. This meant diving into outside storage sheds and coal holes, rummaging through old sacks, garden tools and buckets until the chariots could be hauled out.

Tommy found his soon enough. It hadn't been used since last year and the runners had begun to rust. No matter; they would still glide over the packed snow and the woodwork was firm and dry.

The first slalom was down Camden Street itself, from the junction with Bradshaw Street almost to the main road. The sledges needed a good push to start them, which also meant a nifty jump on board as they set off. They gathered speed quite well until the need to slew and brake with one foot digging into the snow in order to steer the sledge to the kerb before hitting the road. Each successive run, which was punctuated by a sweating and tiring haul back up the street, became better as the snow was compacted beneath the iron runners. Fun was short-lived.

"Aw, no!" howled Robert, as he spied Mrs Giddens emerging from her front door with a shovel.

She proceeded to scatter ashes from her fire grate across the street as she stridently remarked, "Clear off and stop turning the street into a deathtrap!"

"A deathtrap?" muttered Tommy.

"Old people have to get to the shop you know," continued Mrs G by way of explanation, "and my Stan needs to be able to park his car. He won't be able to drive up the street if you keep making it slippy." Just because they owned one of only three cars on the street... Anyway, Mr Calvert had a car but he wasn't grumbling. He could of course park it on the backstreet when it wasn't in the garage, but that was beside the point in Tommy's view.

This served to encourage the children to venture further afield, literally. They headed for the Hard Platts, a huge spread of sloping, open land a quarter of a mile away. This provided a much better run of several hundred yards, though it meant a long haul back to the top. It wasn't a very efficient slide down the grassy part, but there was a path which ran from top to bottom. Keeping to this meant a good downhill run reaching giddy speeds before ending at the fence which marked the boundary of the railway line.

Several children came to grief crashing into the fence before they could halt their hurtling run. No one was hurt –

at least not much – though several spars of fencing became loosened.

The splendid fun drew to a close as twilight descended and the distant street lights began to emit an amber glow. Sledges were dragged and scraped along behind weary and damp but happy children. Roaring fires at home would soon thaw them out.

Spring and Easter

There were several days in late winter and early spring that kept the thermometer languishing and coal rations dwindling. The children at St Joseph's even got the bonus of an unexpected holiday when the school boiler burst. It was mended all too soon for their liking, however, and the drudgery of school work went on.

Soon it was time for the austerity of Lent. All the children had trooped out of the yard and up the stairs for the Ash Wednesday Mass. They duly received a smudge of damp ashes on their foreheads while the priest mournfully intoned that they needed to remember their mortality.

Tommy's Lenten resolution was the typically unoriginal one of giving up sweets. Pennies thus saved were to be handed in at school. Each child had a St Joseph's penny card. Surrounding a likeness of the man himself was a border of squares. For every penny donated, the teachers would pierce a square with a pin, the aim being to have a completely punctured card by Easter. Needless to say, the cards were held by the teachers to avoid anyone succumbing to the temptation of over stabbing.

Tommy was still treated to sweets at home – the only snag being that he wasn't allowed access to them. Instead, he was "encouraged" to place them in the cupboard in the living room. The torture of such deprivation, and how exquisitely it was heightened by this action, had its consolation in the sure and certain knowledge that, come Easter, an almighty binge was in prospect.

The Easter season also brought with it another obligation on all good Catholics; that of fulfilling their Easter duties as ordered by the Church. This meant even more frequent Confession as well as the weekly Communion. It was hardly a time to consider sinning more frequently, so Tommy, along with many other children, felt obliged to "invent" some sins in order to satisfy the priest at Confessional. At least, that was the strategy he adopted after trying to convince the priest (on the advice of his teacher, it has to be said) that he was sinless and had only come to Confession in order to receive a blessing.

On that particular occasion he was sent packing forth-with from the confessional box in order to *"examine his conscience more carefully"*. One didn't argue the issue with Father Lister, but made oneself scarce lest he should ascertain the identity of the bold individual who would challenge the authority of the Church.

At last Holy Week had arrived with its promise of Easter joy, not least another holiday. On Good Friday the Calvert family indulged in their annual pilgrimage to North Wales. They had travelled down to Nanna Hannah's on the Thursday evening to stop overnight before the next leg of the journey. This would take them to Holywell and Pantasaph.

Setting off from Nanna's at 12.30 in the afternoon, they soon reached the centre of Liverpool – traffic being much lighter on the non-working day – and headed for the Mersey Tunnel. This was always a thrill for Tommy, driving underneath the great River Mersey while above them were ships passing to and fro, including the ferry boats that he had been on more than once with his auntie. Eventually they emerged from the gloom of the tunnel into bright sunshine at Birkenhead.

Picking their way out of the town, which was a smaller mirror image of the industrial sprawl of its far-bank city neighbour, they passed through the Wirral and met the crossroads of Queensferry. Taking the coastal route, they soon entered Wales with its twin language road signs.

There was time to visit the shrine of St Winifred at Holywell. They trooped out of the car to see the outdoor pool where pilgrims would come to bathe. The best bit for Tommy was the covered archway at the end which housed a deep pool of water from which there was a constant up-welling of a spring. It was reputed that Winifred herself was beheaded at this spot and that her severed head had rolled onto the spot at which the spring had miraculously risen. There was even a dark stain beneath the water which just might have been some of her blood.

Suitably chastened, the party set off for the last short stretch to the monastery at Pantasaph. Here they would join other pilgrims for a Calvary journey with the monks. First it was time to repair to the hall staffed by local good ladies and in which could be purchased a reviving cup of tea and a hot cross bun – just the thing for devout churchgoers.

Suitably refreshed, they flocked outside for the trudge uphill to the start of the procession. Slightly overdue, several monks appeared bearing a crucifix on a long pole. They led the procession up the hill where they would pause at each of the fourteen Stations of the Cross that the monks had faithfully built along the steep path.

Once at the summit, and with all fourteen Stations complete, the abbot leading the service took the opportunity to deliver an appropriate sermon to his captive congregation. Tommy carefully glanced around him and noted the splendid view afforded over the boundary wall of the abbey. Rolling countryside and distant Welsh peaks made him envious of those travelling free without feeling the need to undergo the penance endured by the present company.

A fresh breeze had sprung up as if to remind those present that it was still only March. Dressed in only a shirt and light jumper, Tommy was distinctly feeling the cold. It was none too soon when, at last, the homily was over and the impatient crowd was able to scramble back down the path to civilisation.

Never was the inside of the car a more welcoming refuge than now, as the shivering Calvert family clambered aboard. They set off back to Liverpool and Tommy was asleep before they had reached Queensferry.

Another night was spent at Grandma's. There was time in the morning for Aunt Marie to again make a fuss of Tommy and Shirley by producing two splendid Easter eggs. The children accepted them gratefully but were reminded by their mum that they couldn't contemplate opening them until Easter day itself. That meant the eggs would have to join the growing pile of sweet goodies that had been hoarded away over Lent.

On Easter morning the family had a lie-in after their travels. This meant that instead of attending their usual nine o clock Mass, they would be going to the eleven o'clock service along with all the other slovens. This meant an even longer service, but at least Tommy wasn't obliged to serve at the Mass on this occasion. As the congregation spilled out onto Macleod Street, the scene was reminiscent of that after the Christmas Midnight Mass, except that it was in daylight.

There were the exchanges of greetings and, to the delight of the young, handing over of Easter eggs. Tommy acquired two more via this ceremony. How on earth was he going to manage them all on top of the mound of sweets he had accumulated since Ash Wednesday? It wasn't a problem that caused him a great deal of worry, however.

As the following day was also a Bank Holiday, Mr and Mrs Calvert decided that a run out into the country would be a good idea. Tommy, anticipating a day of captivity in the back of the car with nothing to help him pass the time, asked if they could take Robert along with them. Much to Shirley's disgust, his mum and dad agreed. Tommy at once sprinted out of the house to inform his best pal of the good news.

He never gave it a thought that Robert's parents might have made plans of their own. As it happened, they had. Since this involved visiting Robert's grandparents, who lived close by, and in view of the fact that Robert had both a brother and a sister who would be company for the elders, Robert was granted leave to go with the Calverts.

At eight thirty the following morning, Tommy was downstairs ready for the off, only to discover that his mum had started even earlier and was packing away the picnic food for the trip. Tommy had to sprint up the street to fetch his pal while Dad was packing the car boot. Luckily, Robert's mum and dad had ensured that he was ready. On their return, they discovered that Shirley was already encased in the rear offside seat of the Austin 10. The two boys had to squeeze alongside her. Shirley insisted that Tommy take the middle of the seat. Much as she detested the close company of her brother, she certainly didn't want to have to sit next to his stupid friend.

It had been decided that they would drive to North Yorkshire for their outing, going first to the market town of Settle before exploring further afield.

Parking the car in the market square, Dad and Mum decided, much to the disgust of Tommy and Robert, to wander round the village shops.

"Why did we have to stop here?" grumbled Tommy to his pal.

Robert didn't know what he was expected to offer by way of a reply. After all, it was Tommy's mum and dad who had made the decision.

"There's nothing here – only shops!" added Tommy, as if to strengthen his case.

"I expect we'll be going soon," offered Robert.

"I hope so," was the heartfelt response.

Sure enough, the parental perambulation came to an end

and, with everyone fairly comfortably settled in, they pulled out of the square and headed north. Passing through the quaintly named village of Giggleswick, they soon reached Clapham Common. The spirits of the boys began to lift. At last they were in open country! Perhaps they would stop somewhere where there was room to play.

Mr Calvert pulled off the road onto the open common consisting of turf and reeds. Tommy and Robert literally tumbled out of the car and ran around the field until they had explored it sufficiently. Returning to the car they pestered Mr Calvert, who was trying to set up the picnic, until he extricated a football from the car boot.

Whooping with joy, Tommy gave the ball a hefty boot and the two lads set off in pursuit. It was hardly a suitable setting for football, but they made the most of the conditions. Eventually, they settled for drop-kicking the ball to one another in order to by-pass the tufts of reeds and the sheep droppings.

The rest of the family, meanwhile, had spread a rug on the ground and had set about the preparation of the simple meal. As well as sandwiches, a flask and cake, there was a fine bacon and egg pie that Mrs C had specially prepared the night before.

When Robert was offered a piece, he was rather dubious. He liked bacon and egg, but what was it doing in a pie? In the event, he was judged wise to be uncertain.

Tommy eagerly received a slice of the pie and took a hearty bite. Seconds later he spat it out with a cry of, "*Yeeurgh!*"

"What did you do that for?" admonished Shirley.

"It's horrible!"

"That's not a very nice thing to say when Mum took the trouble to make it."

"Well, you have a taste then," retorted Tommy.

Shirley could hardly back down after defending Mum.

She took a tentative nibble before admitting that something wasn't right. It turned out that Mrs Calvert had used sugar for the seasoning instead of salt. She was mortified on realising her error but Dad, loyal to the last, came to the rescue.

"I'll have some," he offered, and to the amazement of the children, he ate a large slice with apparent relish.

Somewhat in awe, the boys silently chewed through their ham and tomato sandwiches, followed by a slice of chocolate cake with chocolate butter cream. Mrs Calvert's culinary reputation was restored. Meal over, the impromptu football session resumed until it was time to pile back into the car. The trip wasn't over yet, however.

They drove on a few miles until they reached the village of Clapham. There they disgorged once more. The village itself took only five minutes to exhaust. Then they headed out towards, as the signs proclaimed, the famous cave. A walk of about one and a half miles through woods and meadow led them to the cave entrance.

After paying at the kiosk, they had to wait for a while until the previous tour was complete and the guide was ready to lead them through. Entering the dark and damp recess, they soon had to duck their heads in order to negotiate the passage.

To the amusement of the boys, Shirley became quite concerned about her ability to continue without spoiling her appearance. Their attention was soon diverted by their fascination with the interior of the cave.

There was a distinct, malodorous atmosphere, heightened by the steady dripping of water penetrating through the cave roof. This made a hollow echo as it splashed onto the cave floor. Added to this was the film of slime which coated the walls and floor, making it necessary for the party to tread with care along the passage.

At the far reach of the cave tour, the guide had one

further experience in store. Instructing the group to duck their heads, he led them along a low section where they were required to virtually bend double in order to pass through. When they were assembled in a wider and taller section of the cave, he said that they were going to experience total darkness. Then he turned off a switch and plunged them into a complete blackout. Tommy held out his hand in front of his face and was fascinated by the fact that he couldn't see it. Not at all.

When the light was turned back on, everyone gave a sigh of relief.

Robert whispered, "I wouldn't like to stop down here on my own."

"Nor me," gasped Tommy.

The bright sunlight caused them all to blink when they emerged out into the open some minutes later. The walk back down to the car was considerably easier. After a brief spell playing round the stream, they climbed back into the car again for the journey home.

Summer Fun

The coming summer was the last that Tommy would enjoy in the confined world of his junior days. He had passed the eleven-plus, which meant that he had gained a place in the nearest Catholic secondary school. The nearest such was situated twelve miles away in Blackburn. None of his school pals would be joining him, nor any of the friends he regularly played with. One or two of these were bright enough, but as they were not of his faith they would be able to attend the local technical school up the hill. The others would go to one of the secondary moderns.

Before the need to worry about such changes in his life, there was plenty for Tommy to immerse himself in during his final term. There was cricket – he had made the school team this season – and bathing at the outdoor pool in the park during the hot weekends of June and early July.

There were regular outings into the countryside when Mr Calvert drove the family around Lancashire and into the Yorkshire Dales. Best of all, though, were the expeditions undertaken by the gang of local lads who regularly met on Bradshaw Street by Atkins' shop.

A funfair was coming to Nelson during the week before the local Wakes fortnight began. While the money situation was fairly tight as some of them were accruing spending money for their own family's holidays, a visit was imperative.

They decided to venture down to the spare land adjacent to Victoria Park where the fair had been set up. This meant a hike across town, but such distances were well within the scope of the group, once they had obtained parental permission. The safety of numbers persuaded the more reluctant adults that their offspring would be fine.

Robert had brought along his cousin who, with his family, was visiting the area. There were the usual suspects – Brian, Ronnie, Eric, Dave and Alec. They met as arranged straight after tea, after assuring their parents that they would be home by about half eight. By that time their money would be exhausted anyway.

By the time the excited group of eight lads crossed the canal bridge and headed down Carr Road, they were part of a growing throng of youths of both sexes, some with their parents and most seeming older than their gang of eleven and twelve-year-olds.

They could hear the strident piping music as they neared their destination. Rounding the last terrace and scrambling down the banking towards the plot, their senses were further stimulated by the garish colours and the flashing lights of the stalls. Added to this was the aroma of onions, candyfloss, potatoes, popcorn and goodness knows what else, all deliciously mingled in an invisible cloud which drifted over the whole show. Racing across the cinders, they merged with the tide of people lapping at the entrances and to-ing and fro-ing as their fancy took them.

The boys decided, unwisely, to invest some of their spending money in an effort to increase their resources at the Roll A Penny stall. Actually, Robert and Dave managed to come away with more pennies than they outlayed. The others decided to budget carefully from then on, with the obvious exception of Ronnie. He felt it necessary to sustain himself with a bag of sweets and a choc ice, even thought it wasn't long since they had all had tea.

The waltzer was the first big ride to attract them. They stood watching for a while. There was the usual show-off (presumably a relative of the ride owner) in the form of a young man straddling the moving and undulating deck. He was both collecting fares and chatting up the girls on the ride whilst balancing with ease as the cars began to accelerate round. He found time to spin one or two of the cars around to elicit shrieks before leaping to the central control area.

A few of the lads waited patiently for the gyrating cars to slow and stop. Then they pushed forward and claimed a couple of cars before anyone else could beat them to it. By then, Tommy and Robert (with cousin) had moved on to explore further afield. They came to a big wheel but this seemed to take too long to change passengers and get going again. They arrived at the rockets just as they were slowing and descending, so they clung to the edge of the platform and railing surrounding the ride.

As the rockets grounded, and before the previous occupants could disembark, they laid hands on the fuselages to claim them. Robert had to go with his cousin, of course, so Tommy got in the front seat of the rocket behind theirs. He found that a large woman had deposited her young child in the seat behind his.

Oh, well, I won't have to look at him, thought Tommy, I just hope he doesn't start crying.

They paid their fares. With a jerk, the rockets began to rotate. Picking up speed, they then started to rise up, only to descend partway. The ride continued thus, with the rockets rising and falling at an ever increasing speed. Robert tried to turn around to wave at Tommy but then had to clutch at the bar in front of him for balance. The boys' hair was blown back by the rush of wind.

By now, the rest of the fair was a blur of colour and noise, except for the times when the rockets rose until only sky and rooftops could be seen. The feeling was exhilarating, added to by a queasy sensation whenever the rockets swooped on their downward path. All too soon, they stopped rising and gradually slowed and sunk to ground level.

The ride was over. With slightly wobbly legs, the boys emerged laughing and chattering as they regrouped. They met with two more of their mates and headed for the helter-skelter. This seemed to offer decent value for money.

For tuppence each they were issued with a coconut mat and informed that they could have three goes. This involved a frantic climb up the winding stairs inside the tower. Once on top, they had to perch on the narrow launching platform and arrange themselves on their piece of matting. This wasn't easy as the people behind pushed forward and barged into them. Inevitably, they set off only half on the mat, with legs flailing the air. Bumping around the far from regular curves on the shiny slope, they eventually tumbled out at the bottom before being cannoned in to by the one behind. Robert was the one cannoning in to Tommy, so that was all right.

At the risk of further damage to clothing and limbs, they scurried back up for their remaining two goes.

Next up were the galleries – the rifle range and the coconut shies. Brian duly informed them that the coconut stall was a cheat because each coconut was supported by a back piece so that it couldn't be knocked off its base. Certainly, they didn't see many coconuts being hit, let alone one becoming dislodged. The bank of cuddly toys and other prizes looked alarmingly complete and undisturbed. Thus discouraged, they moved on.

Now the rifle range was a different matter. Skill counted here. By resting elbows on the counter, squinting at the target cards and holding breath while squeezing the trigger, it was possible to direct a pellet at the centre of the card. At least that's where the slug should have ended up. Most only nicked the outer edges of the cards while some missed altogether.

Of course, Brian had a theory for this as well. The barrels of the air rifles were very slightly bent, weren't they, or else the sights on top had been misaligned. That didn't explain how the lad next to them managed to win a prize, unless his miss-aim had counterbalanced the variation in flight. Brian's deduction again. Well, he had to justify his theory.

Funds were getting low now so it was time for a rethink and a pause in the spending. They spotted a booth which proclaimed itself to contain not one, not two but three amazing sights. There was a bearded lady, a snake man and a pair of human monkey twins. While the boys were not convinced by these ridiculous claims, they were nevertheless curious to found out just how the owners of the booth proposed to convince their customers. They weren't curious enough to waste their precious money, however. Dave came up with an alternative plan. They would sneak round the back of the tent.

Having decided to do this, they had to take a long route round so as not to arouse suspicion. They went right to the end of the line of stalls and tents. Ducking into the park bushes at the back, they made their way to the rear of the booth in question. Tiptoeing carefully over the guy ropes and folded canvas, they dropped to the ground and carefully began to lift a stretch of canvas forming the back wall of the tent. This wasn't easy as there was a considerable layer of canvas on the ground and it was quite heavy, pegged down as it was to both sides of the section they were manipulating.

Lying completely flat, by twisting sideways and wriggling forward, Tommy managed to get his head underneath the fold. His friends had gone quiet. Taking advantage of the silence, he pushed his head forward until he could peer up a little. He managed to see the back of a female figure perched on a chair. She had long dark curly hair and was wearing a blue velvet dress.

Before he could see any more detail, he both heard a gruff voice and felt his legs being pulled from behind. He emerged blinking and rolled onto his back to be met by a fearful figure.

An angry looking man with rolled-up sleeves and deeply tanned, bulging arms bellowed at him, "What d'yer think you're up to? Do you want me to fetch the police?"

"S–sorry, mister, I were only having a quick look," replied a shaken Tommy, looking to his friends for corroboration. They had scarpered, it seemed, leaving him to the wrath of this ogre.

"If you ain't got any money, clear off before I give yer a good clip, like you deserve!" threatened the ogre.

Tommy quite believed he would do, so he cleared off with haste, pausing only as he tripped over a guy rope. When he emerged sweating round the front of the stalls, he was met by a most unsympathetic group of his pals chortling at his misfortune.

"You might have warned me," he rounded on them.

"We couldn't, honest! He came round the corner too quick," said Robert, sounding convincing.

Calm was restored when Ronnie offered Tommy a piece of pink rock to crunch on by way of consolation. As if in deference to the much mollified Tommy, they veered away from the troublesome area of the stalls and booths and headed across to the rides. Disdaining the tame roundabouts that were obviously designed with much younger children in mind, they wandered over to the tall structure that seemed to be the cause of much screaming.

Arriving at the source of this disturbance, they glanced skywards. Their gazing took in a huge steel arm which was bolted through the centre and radiated in opposite directions with one side pointing upwards and the other towards the ground. At each end of the arm was a capsule that housed four people. They noted the attention that this ride was getting from everyone so they decided to join the queue.

At the start of each session, the car at the bottom of the arm loaded with customers. It was then set in motion until it reached the top and the other car was at the bottom. This was also loaded up. The boys couldn't help but notice that, during this activity, the people placed in the first capsule were left suspended upside down some fifty feet in the air.

"Flippin' heck!" gasped Dave, somewhat unnecessarily as the occupants of the upper car made their presence felt by a combined screaming and moaning sound.

The cage of the lower car was slammed shut and further gasps and groans were lost as the whole arm began to rotate at increasing speed. The cries of the occupants rose and fell as they were whirled round. Several upturned boys' faces gaped in open-mouthed fascination as they witnessed the exhilaration and terror of the riders.

"I'm not going in that!" declared Ronnie before anyone could suggest otherwise.

I feel the same, thought Tommy to himself, before adding out loud, "I'm not so sure…"

"Go on," urged Robert, "it'll be a laugh. I dare you."

By this time they had neared the front of the queue and would be going on the ride after the next go. Tommy would gladly have joined Ronnie, who by now had retreated to the safety of the hoop-la stall. However, the rest of his friends were eagerly pressing forward and it would have taken more courage to defy them and drop out of line. So he accepted his fate and, at the next change over, allowed himself to be half pushed into the car.

The man in charge clanged shut the protective cage and retreated to the booth to press the switch. As he felt the ride set in motion with a slight jerk, Tommy gripped the restraining bar tightly until his knuckles turned white. He cared not that Robert seemed to be relaxing and had clasped his hands nonchalantly behind his head.

Dave and Eric were also sharing the car. It wasn't long before they were all hanging on and shutting their eyes each time they span upwards. All they could do was gasp breathlessly as they hurtled over and round time and time again. With relief, they felt the ride slowing down. It wasn't over yet though. They were left suspended upside down while the other car was emptied. With a final plunge, they swooped down and were released none too soon.

"That was great, wasn't it?" cried Dave after he had reeled away from the platform.

Yeah, thought Tommy, but please don't say let's have another go!

Luckily, their money had run out. Actually they managed to scrape enough together for a final treat. Robert and Tommy pooled their last pennies to purchase a large ball of candy floss which they ate by alternate bites. Dave and Eric shared a toffee apple, which succumbed to their eager crunching. Soon all four of them were engaged in licking off the sticky sugar and toffee residue from around their lips. A final wipe with the sleeve which was then rubbed on the back of the pants completed the process of ablution.

Chattering drunkenly, they hurried back up Carr Road. It was just beginning to grow a little dusky, though this was exaggerated by the bright lights of the fair. Having asked a passer-by for the time and been told it was nearly 8.25 p.m., they broke in to a run. The last of them reached home just after 8.40, in time to receive a gentle reprimand from relieved parents.

Growing Up

It was during this very seminal summer that Tommy experienced a couple of events that would remain in his memory for some time.

The first of them began innocuously enough. Robert, his older brother Alec, Dave, Jimmy and Tommy were afoot. The gang were strolling along the path between the allotments which bounded the Hard Platts. Rounding a corner, they encountered one of their deadly enemies – Denton, who led a gang that inhabited the other side of the railway tracks. Denton sported the badge of his office – a school cap worn back to front so that the peak stuck out behind. Somehow, the rounded front of the cap, thus worn, gave his forehead a more menacing appearance, emphasising his slightly slanted eyes and beetling brow.

Unfortunately – for Denton, that is – the latter's gang were presently non-existent, apart from his lone companion. Give him his due, with great presence of mind, he abruptly turned and gestured around the corner from which he had emerged, shouting, "Come on lads, let's get 'em!"

This subterfuge didn't fool Tommy's group one bit. Granted this rare opportunity, they prepared to make mincemeat of Denton and Mick, his lone friend. Denton wasn't quite out of ideas yet. He attempted to parley with the lads but his pleas and bargaining fell on unsympathetic ears. It was Mick who came to his rescue. Amazingly, he offered to fight one of his enemies in single combat in order to avert the slaughter that would surely take place otherwise.

Even more amazingly, Alec, acting as the senior and decisive voice, accepted the challenge. He would let one of his charges take Mick on. There was no shortage of volunteers. However, he turned to Tommy. He was curious to find out whether Tommy was worthy as he had never witnessed him in combat.

Tommy was glad to oblige. The others parted to allow space for Mick and Tommy to come to grips. They clashed, grabbing at each other and attempting to wrestle their opponent to the ground.

After a brief scuffle, they fell onto the hard path and rolled around while they sought the upper hand. Mick managed to get Tommy into a headlock. With Tommy's head firmly wedged in the crook of his elbow and his knuckles locked together, Mick began to apply the pressure. Tommy wriggled frantically, twisting and turning as he gasped for breath. He succeeded in kneading his own knuckles into the small of his opponent's back. Mick gasped with pain and released his grip sufficiently for Tommy to wrestle and break free.

The fight was in the balance again. They both staggered to their feet. Arms locked around necks and torsos as they each sought to trip the other boy. Mick half managed it, then, as Tommy stumbled, he twisted and fortuitously managed to drag Mick down with him.

Egged on by the opposing onlookers, they rolled around on the stony dirt path.

It was now a trial of strength. Tommy began to gain the upper hand. They were very much of similar build, but Tommy seemed to be more determined. Perhaps it was the knowledge that the rest of the gang were scrutinising his performance. Whatever, he eventually rolled his opponent onto his back and managed to stay on top. Then he straddled him.

At this point the other lads urged him to go to work with his fists, but Tommy was unused to violence at that level. Instead, he sought the surrender of the other boy by holding him down and asking if he wished to give in.

The other boys, Denton apart, were disappointed that Tommy hadn't exacted a higher price from Mick for his boldness. He still hadn't conceded defeat despite being firmly pinned to the ground. Tommy remembered a move that ought to achieve a response. Maintaining his grip on Mick's wrists, he moved first one knee and then another, planting them in the sockets of his victim's shoulder.

At this, Mick gave a sharp cry of pain and gasped, "OK, OK, I give in!" Mercifully, Tommy levered himself away from the pinioned Mick. He felt proud of his swift victory but his elation was not mirrored in the faces of his pals. However, honour had to be seen to be done, so Denton and his aide were released to fight another day. They made a hasty retreat with the jeers of their foes mocking their departure.

The second experience of that summer was to prove far more memorable to Tommy for completely different reasons.

It had been the custom for some time for several of the juniors in the top class to engage in a particular game after school. This involved a short walk in to town by a mixed group of boys and the more bold girls. Their destination was the open market, but only on the afternoons when it wasn't open for business.

On one such afternoon, when the school had disgorged at the end of the day, a group of the top class children headed along Every Street towards their destination. They rounded the corner by the library and continued along Cross Street to find the open market. This was of course shut on this occasion. Though the stalls were barricaded up, there was open access to the warren of alleyways which led between them and which were under cover. When deserted, this was ideal territory for their game of kiss-chase.

Now, it must be said that Tommy was not a part of this regular foray for two reasons. Firstly, the route lay in the opposite direction from that leading to Tommy's home and the trip would have made him late. Secondly, and more to the point, he was far from ready to indulge in such activities with fellow schoolmates, or indeed any members of the opposite sex. He wouldn't know where to hide if he ever found himself face to face with a girl in these circumstances. Oh, he could get along fine all right with Stella, unless of course she ever represented a challenge of this nature.

Still, the other lads had pestered Tommy on this particular occasion and urged him to accompany them. He had run out of excuses and felt duty bound, in order to save face, to go with them on this occasion. Perhaps it would be all right. He could just watch or make a token effort to join in. Anyway, he was a good runner and no girl would be able to catch him if he was careful.

Innocently, he entered into the spirit of things. The boys duly gave the girls a head-start before pursuing them around and between the stalls. Tommy watched the other lads eagerly racing after the girls. He sluggishly followed suit. Needless to say, he didn't encounter anyone and so was spared any ordeal.

To his horror, the second round involved role reversal. The boys sped off in order to be flushed out by the girls. The rules were quite clear. No one could stray beyond the enclosed area of the stalls.

Tommy frantically raced to and fro before deciding to hide in a secluded corner, wedged between two of the empty, canvas-draped stalls. He heard the squeals of the others and wondered just who was pursuing whom. Unfortunately, he had not taken part before today and therefore was unaware that his chosen hiding place was well known to the other participants.

Yvonne was the most popular girl in St Joseph's and she never had any difficulty in finding or being caught by the boys. She was therefore out of the equation as she was never allowed to progress to exploring the recesses. But Sheila wasn't. She had played before. Being unable to catch any of the boys as they raced to and fro round the pillars and canopies of the stalls, she decided to explore the corners.

She stumbled upon Tommy almost before he realised. The rules of the game dictated the next move. Lunging forward, Sheila planted a firm kiss full on the surprised mouth of her capture.

Tommy was at first horrified. Then he felt a peculiar shudder of warmth and pleasant surprise coursing through his very being.

It was all over in a moment. Sheila retreated giggling and left a shell-shocked figure rocking back against the back wall of the market area.

Wow! So this is the game, he thought in his bemused state. Wait till I tell Robert!

Thus initiated, Tommy set off to rejoin the group. He was not to encounter Sheila again that afternoon, or indeed to find himself in another such situation, partly to his relief. The party had broken up and everyone was heading for home before they had some explaining to do to account for their lateness.

Tommy didn't remember his journey homeward that day. It would be a long time before he got over his experience and he would never look upon girls in quite the same way again.

Moving On

That summer was to prove the longest in Tommy's memory. Actually there were several valid reasons for this. For a start, the weather turned out to be even more dire than usual. There were seemingly endless days of persistent rain; rain which lasted throughout most of the day and precluded any outdoor pursuit. These were days on which Tommy was forced to revert to his button collection in order to pass the frustrating daylight hours.

On top of this, he was due to transfer to secondary school. He had gained a place in the nearest Catholic grammar school, which just happened to be in Blackburn. This would not only mean a lengthy journey by train but a complete severance from all of his best friends and local playmates. No one else from St Joseph's would be making that journey with him.

It was as if all the lads around realised that Tommy was somehow different now. They accepted his Roman faith – indeed it was never a topic of conversation – but the fact that he would not be growing into teenage and then manhood with them seemed to create a barrier to further friendship.

They would be able to discuss their mutual future prospects. Whose class would they end up in? Would they be in the same one that their older brother had attended? Would their older brothers protect them in the dangerous world of the big playgrounds? Who would they walk to school with?

Tommy had no one in whom to confide such thoughts or with whom to share his apprehension. While *they* could take comfort from their shared concern, he could only look ahead to a guaranteed uncertainty.

To add to all this, he was facing up to the longest summer break ever. Junior school had broken up for the Wakes fortnight, which marked the start of the long holidays, at the end of June. While his erstwhile classmates and friends could anticipate a return to their education in mid-August, he had to await the autumn term pattern for Blackburn. This meant that schools would not resume until early September.

Eight weeks' holiday – surely paradise found! Not so. As well as the inclement, not to say dreary, weather, he would have no one for company during the last two weeks.

At least there was the Calvert summer holiday safari to occupy the first two weeks. This time the venue was East Cornwall – a holiday caravan park on the Channel coast. The weather proved to be rather better than the norm for East Lancashire throughout that season. This only caused Tommy even more frustration when they returned to Nelson's leaden skies.

On the first dry day after their return, Tommy hurried up Camden Street to renew acquaintances with his lifelong pals. Some had been away for the fortnight, some for a week and some not at all. This didn't seem to create any division or jealousies. After all, it was the same situation every year.

Eagerly, Tommy walked up to the group of boys gathered, as usual, on the corner by Atkin's.

"Hiya! what yer doin'?"

"Nothin' much."

"Just wondering about the football. How Burnley are going to do next season."

"Talking about next year at Walverden secondary."

That last remark was tantamount to shutting the door in Tommy's face. What had he got in common with his mates now? He couldn't discuss his school with them. They wouldn't be interested. They wouldn't care less about his concerns. What had that to do with them?

With sinking heart, Tommy levered himself onto the garden wall near the edge of the group. There he sat, listening but unable to join in. Part of the clan, but somehow remotely removed from their futures. Robert at least was still chatting to him. But for how much longer? How soon before he too recognised that they were travelling down widely diverging paths?

He was a good mate, Robert. The best ever. But from now on Tommy would have to seek out new acquaintances. He would have to mix with other young lads from Colne, Brierfield, Burnley and goodness knows where.

How could he play with such friends in the evenings? Of course, he couldn't. But how could he play with his old friends? They would be home from school much sooner than he. They would not have so much homework to fill their weekday evenings. They would have been strengthening their bonds of friendship throughout the day while he was meeting new faces.

As if this wasn't agony enough for the despondent lad, he was hauled off on the train in order to procure his uniform. The only supplier of this was John Forbes' outfitter's near King George's Hall in Blackburn. Thus Mrs Calvert was required to accompany Tommy on her day off. They took the 9.45 train from Nelson station, arriving in Blackburn some thirty-five minutes later. It was the local service operating to Preston and stopping at all stations en route.

Alighting onto the boulevard at Blackburn, Mrs Calvert immediately sought directions to Gray's. Towing a less than enthusiastic Tommy in her wake, she strode out past the Cathedral and through the shopping arcade. Being of single mind, she didn't pause to view the wares on display.

It took a little over five minutes' steady striding to reach the outfitter's. There Tommy was prodded, measured and garmented by the angular figure of the shop manager, who was clearly well versed in kitting out the novitiates.

He was soon clothed in a navy blazer with pale blue piping and the crest of the Marist College of St Mary's adorning the breast pocket. Mrs Calvert beamed proudly but Tommy felt rather less than enthusiastic as the shopkeeper completed the image by pulling a school cap firmly down on his crown. Tommy was invited to walk to the full-length mirror. He couldn't help but feel slightly ridiculous as his sleeves reached down to his fingertips. The peak of his cap hid his curly locks and only a bare forehead topped a somewhat moon-like visage.

Would he have to wear this outfit every day? How would he be able to walk past his old pals? He knew it was pointless to express an opinion. He would simply have to get used to his new image.

The journey back home on the train became a voyage of gloom. The dark, millstone grit walls and houses of Burnley, Brierfield and Nelson reflected Tommy's image of despondency. No more the laughing streets of his childhood. No more the carefree green fields wherein his imagination frolicked.

There was still a week to go before Tommy's baptism of fire. One more week to savour his freedom before succumbing to the rigours of a grammar school education for ever. What use would that be? His friends were already back at their new schools. They would know by now what it was like to enter the big world. They would be able to regale him with embellished tales of their experiences.

The last days dragged by. On the Thursday, Tommy decided to stroll to the top of Hibson Road for no particular reason. OK, so it happened to be about four o'clock. Perhaps the pupils from the secondary school – the "tech" – would be making their way home any second. Hadn't Stella just started at the tech two weeks ago?

Of course, that had nothing to do with the fact that Tommy fancied a stroll this afternoon. With thoughts of his own immediate future running through his mind – how would he find his way to school? What would the teachers be like? Would he be able to cope? Could he manage the first day? – he had arrived at the end of Bentley Street.

This was where it emerged onto Hibson Road. Yes, there were some boys and girls from the tech coming down the hill now. Tommy decided to make a discreet withdrawal some twenty yards back where he wouldn't be so conspicuous. He hauled himself up onto a garden wall from where he dangled and swung his legs as nonchalantly as he could manage. All the while he scrutinised the passing throngs.

After about four or five minutes, he spotted her. Yes, that was Stella, wasn't it? Walking down on the opposite side with another girl. Should he shout to get her attention? What would he say? Would she think he was stupid? By the time he had decided to do something, the two girls had disappeared from view.

Tommy leapt from the wall and sprinted down the backstreet behind the main road. He came out at the next street lower down which ran parallel to Bentley and which also reached the main road. This time he walked in the opposite direction for a few steps, then turned about and headed for Hibson Road just as the two girls hove into view once more.

His luck was in! Stella and her friend had decided to cross the road. They drew up to the kerb watching for the traffic. Tommy risked a wave. Stella's friend noticed him and gave her pal a nudge. Stella looked across. Tommy waved again. Stella waved back – was she looking slightly embarrassed? She was smiling though. Tommy grinned foolishly and waved again.

Of course they weren't actually going to meet. Why would they? What would Tommy say? At least he had seen his best mate among the girls of the tech.

With a sigh, Tommy turned around and headed for

home. What was the use? Hadn't he been set apart from his old friends and schoolmates for ever? Stella's future was not his. Come to that, nor was Robert's, Dave's, Brian's, Ronnie's or anyone else's.

The dreaded day had finally arrived. Tommy was roused early at 6.45. Duly washed and dressed, he was downstairs for the condemned man's breakfast by 7.10. Then it was time to don "the uniform". His tie had been neatly done by Mum – he could knot his own after practising but it wouldn't have been good enough for his first day. Then the blazer was draped over him as if he were a knight being arrayed for combat. How restricting it felt with its long sleeves and cuffs, its lapels and buttons. Finally, as if to complete the image of his misery, the cap was planted firmly on his head and the peak pulled down.

Of course, Tommy gave no outward sign of his apprehension as his satchel was crossed over his shoulder. A kiss on the cheek from Mum and he was ready. Dad had got permission to start work a few minutes later on this special morning, so he was able to accompany Tommy on the walk down to the station.

"You OK, son?" he asked with concern, following this up with some words of advice and encouragement. Tommy beamed in gratitude for Dad's concern by way of reply.

They reached the station in good time and Dad took his farewell, continuing down the road to the Victory factory while Tommy entered the booking office. He walked up the "L" shaped ramp which led to the island platform. As he emerged at the top he could see several other similarly attired youths already standing nervously around outside the waiting room.

Two of these were standing together and looking a little friendlier than the other passengers. They nodded and smiled in Tommy's direction.

Thus encouraged, Tommy strolled over to them and grinned a shy hello.

"Hiya, I'm Frank and this is John," said the taller one who was wearing glasses.

"My name's Tommy," he replied, adding, "which school are you from?"

"St George's," this from the one called John. "What about you?"

"I went to St Joseph's," answered Tommy, at once realising that his junior days were past and he was now a small fish in a very large secondary pond. What's more, he didn't even have a pal for company as these two did.

Further despondent thoughts were shut away as a distant whistle and then an ever noisier metallic rattle heralded the imminent arrival of their transport. Appearing round the curving track from the direction of Colne grew the coal-black, hissing locomotive with its trail of largely empty carriages. This was the important service to the capital, as announced by a railway employee on the platform in ringing tones: "Burnleee, Accrington, Blackburn, Darren, Bolton, Manchester, Stockport and London Eustonnn."

All this was intoned while the locomotive came to a steaming crawl and finally to a halt with squealing brakes. Tommy stared at the rolling stock passing before his eyes, at the few blurred faces at the windows, and also at his own reflection as the shadow from the platform canopy overhead turned the carriage windows into mirrors.

There was by now quite a collection of people gathered in clumps and awaiting a chance to board: a mix of adults going to work, others on a long outing and schoolboys and girls of varying ages and sizes.

Hands seized brass handles, wrenched open the carriage doors and their owners clambered onto the steps and then the aisles. Tommy followed his new companions and they found themselves in a second-class corridor carriage. The three boys slid open a door and squeezed into an empty compartment. It didn't remain empty for long as a tall, suited man with a briefcase joined them.

Tommy sat down, then promptly rose again as he had half sat on his satchel. Frank and John reached up and pushed theirs onto the string-laced luggage rack above the inward-facing seats.

No sooner had they settled down than a piercing whistle followed by a few slamming doors announced that it was time for departure. With another hiss of steam and a jolt, the engine crept away, labouring to haul the eight carriages that were in tow. It soon picked up speed as it clattered past the marshalling yards.

Tommy stared out of the window to see a trackside fence rising and plunging as it followed the contours of the field. This was the Hard Platts – the large, allotment fringed field upon which he had spent many a blissful afternoon with his friends. He settled back in his seat to the rhythm of the clicking rails, a tune which altered in pitch almost immediately as the train slowed ready to pick up more passengers at Brierfield station.

There were more collections of school children, some neatly scrubbed and in shiny uniform (the nervous first-dayers like Tommy and his new mates), some more nonchalant and casually dressed though still reluctant (the experienced ones).

The boys were to learn that, of the ones not dressed like themselves, the boys would be going to the private grammar school of Queen Elizabeth and the girls in green to the Notre Dame Convent School. They would also soon learn that those other boys were to be regarded as rivals and to be christened with the nickname of "QEGS".

The train made similar stops at all the stations en route to Blackburn and the number of passengers swelled at each one. Quite a few adults, though, alighted at Blackburn along with the pupils. The time was a little after 8.30. The boys passed through the ticket turnstile and emerged to the grey daylight of the boulevard concourse. There awaited a fleet of buses to ferry them to their destinations.

The journey led them through the centre of town, up past the municipal park and onto the crest of the hill where stood the college. Frank and John had allowed Tommy to remain in their company. He was grateful for the common bond that had drawn them together. Feeling a little apprehensive still but buoying each other up, they followed the stream of humanity through the school gates.

They were directed to the main hall.

First Day at Secondary School

There was a considerable amount of noise at first as they were shepherded in to approximate ranks by dint of arm waving and gesturing from gowned staff and senior pupils. After several minutes of organised confusion the shuffling, chattering and coughing subsided quite abruptly. Hundreds of pairs of eyes looked up to see a tall figure in black, ankle-length clerical garb stride to the centre of the stage. He engaged in brief discussion with a bespectacled and gowned staff member before turning to face the newcomers.

"Good morning to you all," were his opening words, followed by a brief pause. This was to allow for the response.

"Morning, Father," rang out raggedly from the ranks.

Seeming satisfied with this, the voice continued: "Welcome to St Mary's College where I hope you are all going to be happy. My name is Father Grey and I am the Principal." He went on to offer more information to the attendant and, in many cases, open-mouthed faces.

Tommy looked around as much as he dared, taking in the windows set high on both side walls. As well as the usual religious artefacts there were large boards containing dates and names. He managed to pay attention while Father Grey explained that these contained the details of past pupils who had graduated from various universities.

"Now I expect that you will all want to know which class you are in."

At this point he gestured for the form teachers to gather with him on the stage. Each one held a register and they took it in turns to recite the names of the pupils who would be in their class. The classes would be named 1X, 1Y and

1Z. This was because they were of equal stature and this titling avoided the erroneous assumption that would have suggested some sort of streaming had the letters A, B and C been used. Nevertheless, Tommy found to his dismay that neither Frank nor John would be in his form, the two of them having been paired in 1Y whilst he was in 1X.

He would be alone again among strangers. What was worse, other boys in the first-year classes seemed to gather in twos, threes and fours. They had obviously moved up from the same junior schools, the majority of which were local schools.

After the welcoming assembly, they were allowed out into the fresh air for a few minutes and to the cloakrooms where many were ready to pay a visit after their first day trauma. Their relief was soon over and they were once more herded into lines.

Class by class they were moved into the corridor of Prospect House. There they had to queue on the narrow, musty stairwell of the old brick building that apparently was the original school.

When it was the turn of 1X, Tommy shuffled along in line behind a blonde-haired boy from Padiham who had travelled in by bus. He was nervous and shy as well, but seemed a nice lad. His name was David and he would become quite a close friend of Tommy's whenever they were together at school. Of course, he would still be able to meet up with Frank and John at break-times and on the journeys to and from Nelson.

Any further musing was curtailed as they were ushered into a circle around the perimeter of the upstairs room. Into their midst strode the formidable figure of Mr Shawbridge, the senior history master. Of course they wouldn't be making his acquaintance as eager pupils. Their early education would be the responsibility of junior masters while the esteemed Mr Shawbridge had much loftier duties which restricted his input to the senior boys.

He was on this occasion wearing another hat, one which he obviously viewed with a degree of distaste. To him fell the task of equipping the fresh intake with the wherewithal of their learning needs. He was giving out the textbooks.

Notwithstanding his aversion towards this menial duty, he approached the task with his usual aplomb. Clasping his hands behind his back and underneath the flowing tails of his academic gown, he strutted to and fro. With spectacles perched on the bridge of his not inconsiderable nose, he exhorted them to treat these treasures with the utmost care.

"You will find inside the front cover a label," he intoned, "upon which you are to write your name and that of your form as well as the date."

He said this as some of his fawning senior students passed round clutching armfuls of weighty grammars and primers. These they deposited none too gently at the feet of each boy.

"You will furthermore look after these books with great care so as to prolong their life. You must bind them with a protective cover which is to bear the title. The books must at all times be available at school on the day of the lessons for which they are needed," he concluded.

Tommy viewed the growing pile of textbooks at his feet with considerable concern. Mr Shawbridge's final words on the subject served only to increase this concern.

"At the end of the academic year you will be required to hand back each book that is finished with. You are account-able, of course, for any undue wear and tear to which the books are subjected and you will be required to contribute towards a replacement."

With this he strode imperiously from the room, with arms still tucked behind his waistband.

The new pupils, already much chastened, looked down with dismay at their individual piles of literature. No one seemed to have a book that looked anything like new, and

149

many of them were already the worse for wear, being of several years' vintage. Tommy's Latin primer had a spine that had been repaired once with tape and glue by the look of it. Flipping open its thick front cover, he discovered that it was originally the temporary property of one Chris Williams of form 1Z in 1951–'52! There were four other names penned below his.

The space where Tommy would scrawl his name was almost at the bottom of the gummed label. So this book had been carried to and fro in satchels, propped open in classrooms and flung onto the floor of Prospect House for the last six years. No doubt old Shawbridge would expect it to rejuvenate itself when it came time to be handed back in.

Taking great care, rather belatedly in the case of most books, the boys pushed their "new" acquisitions into the recesses of their school bags. Then it was time to troop out to make acquaintance with their form rooms and masters. They were issued with exercise books and a jotter, into which they could copy down lesson and homework timetables from the blackboard. Tommy had never experienced homework before.

They were also introduced to the school rules and disciplinary system. The latter consisted of a table of grading, whereby weekly marks were awarded for effort, or the lack of, and behaviour. Any pupil with a surfeit of "D" grades, normally the lowest, would be subject to detention and possibly corporal punishment. This would be automatic if a dreaded "E" grade appeared on the report. B and A grades, extremely rare, could counteract Ds and Es. Thus one's average grade had to amount to a C in order to avoid the above chastisements.

The form master of 1X, Mr Norman, introduced his new charges to education grammar school style by treating them to a Latin lesson. Since none of the boys, fresh out of junior school as they were, had an inkling of the classics, he may as well have delivered a starter lesson in ancient Egyptian hieroglyphics. Before he lapsed into unconsciousness out of hunger or mental exhaustion, Tommy was mightily relieved to hear the ringing tones of the bell signalling the start of the lunch break.

With head spinning, he emerged from the dusty classroom clutching his school bag and his cap. Having been informed by Mr Norman that the first lunch sitting would include the new intake, he followed the tide towards the dining room. This was at the far end of the building, reached down a long corridor. This block obviously contained the science department, judging by the foul odour emanating from one of the rooms. Good planning that, having the science laboratory fairly adjacent to the kitchens.

At least the toilets were also nearby, should anyone feel the urge to quell a gagging sensation. The stream of would-be diners poured into the washing area to scrub up for their meal. It was here that Tommy spotted Frank and John once again. The trio clung together for moral support and joined the jostling queue.

They managed to find a large table where they could sit together along with another five pupils. There they waited until the lucky master appointed to supervision duty signalled their turn to approach the serving hatch. Clutching knife, fork and spoon they shuffled along the line.

Tommy peered anxiously over the shoulders of the boys in front of him. His anxiety was justified. As he drew level with the first cook's assistant and picked up a plate from the stack, he saw and smelled the dish of the day. It was mincemeat pie, boiled potatoes and cabbage! Furthermore, the pie was festooned with glistening grey slivers of onion.

The mincemeat pie was in effect a square of shortcrust pastry hiding a glutinous mass of the darkest brown meat and gravy. It was to earn the nickname of "slop pie" among the boys.

Tommy trudged stoically back to his seat, thumb embedded in the gravy lapping at the shores of his plate. Frank and John looked equally pleased at their helping. Pudding was slightly less of a disaster, consisting of a slab of chocolate coloured cake swimming in custard. At least Tommy was able to avoid the custard by swiftly withdrawing his plate before the server could tip the contents of her brimming jug over his portion. Hungry as the boys were, they managed to make steady inroads into this culinary masterpiece before their taste buds surrendered.

Then it was out to the playground for a frantic game of tig, dodging in and out of huddles of other boys and avoiding the older pupils, who were endeavouring to conduct a game of football among the rabble. Crossing paths with these larger specimens invited a hefty shove out of their territory.

How Tommy survived the afternoon was a mystery even to himself. There was even a list of spellings and a short French vocabulary to be borne home for evening study. All on the first day.

The method of returning to the station to catch the train home appeared to differ somewhat from the morning journey. Instead of a bus ride, it seemed that the out-of-towners were wont to walk down to the centre. Well, it was a steep descent at first down Shear Brow, which was too steep for the buses to negotiate.

The station was reached after crossing the road, going past the market hall and traversing the boulevard. The train was not due until half past four, so that allowed the best part of half an hour for this walk.

By 4.23 the three boys, along with older pupils and girls from the Convent, plus a couple of QEGS types, were stood about on Platform 3. The train which would deliver them thankfully to the bosom of their homes came squeaking in from the direction of Preston. No grand nationwide express this one. It was a local-line service consisting of just three carriages pulled by an unpretentious tanker locomotive.

As John leant on the large door handle and twisted it open, they surveyed the interior. It was a non-corridor compartment. Leaping aboard, they jumped on the seats causing little clouds of dust to rise up and assail their nostrils.

"Ach, eeurgh!" spluttered Tommy theatrically. "I'm choking!"

"Open the window!" yelled John, and Frank lurched across to the opposite side. He pulled at the wide leather strap which was buttoned to the studs on the door. Releasing it to allow the sash window to slide down, he thrust his head out. Now that the dust-caked window had been lowered, they could see across the rails to the tall, grimy brick wall which shut off the railway from the outside world.

As the train lurched off, the boys, who had the compartment to themselves, realised that they were cocooned in their own little world beyond the reach not only of other passengers but also British Rail staff. Flinging their bags onto the luggage rack, they began to throw themselves about the seats until darkness suddenly descended. They were unfamiliar with the long tunnel which lay just beyond the eastern exit of the station.

The journey home actually took longer on this slower rig but they didn't care. Every mile was taking them nearer home. Rows of brick terraces and factories gave way to dark grey ones of millstone grit. Yes, they were back on familiar territory.

Outside Nelson station, Tommy waved goodbye to Frank and John. They were going up Railway Street to their homes in St George's parish while he would be heading underneath the tunnel and on up Hibson Road.

Oh, well, it wasn't so bad today, apart from my first homework, thought Tommy, and at least I've got some new friends to settle in with.

Loneliness and New Hope

The autumn term became gradually chillier as inexorably as the days grew shorter. The first time Tommy found himself in detention, he also found himself journeying home in the dusk.

The loss of his liberty after the school day was the result of a run-in with old Mrs Hartley, the antiquarian English teacher assigned to form 1X. She had deemed a reply by Tommy to one of her searching questions to be impertinent. It was nothing of the sort, of course – at least not intentionally. But it was enough of an excuse for her to give him a "D" grade. This, as well as one for not having his maths homework handed in on time, was enough to cancel out a good grade for French.

His fate thus sealed, Tommy resigned himself to spending three-quarters of an hour in the company of Mr Taylor of the geography department, along with another eight unfortunates. The plus side was that he was able to make a start on his evening's homework. The minus was that he would miss the 4.30 train home.

He had heard that the next train was due at 5.30: thus he was able to amble down Shear Brow with plenty of time to spare. He made a slight detour in order to visit the chemist's shop at the end of the arcade. Reaching the front door, Tommy fumbled in his pockets to check how much money he had to spare.

Yes, I'll treat myself. I need cheering up after being left to make my way home on my own, he decided, pushing open the shop door.

The kindly face of the bespectacled chemist, someone who obviously appreciated the young, beamed down at him as its owner greeted Tommy with, "And what can I do for you, young man?"

"Twopenny lolly, please. What flavours have you got?"

Tommy had made the detour, rather than going to the sweetshop or newsagents, because he knew that the chemist practised his skills by making his own iced lollies and inventing new flavours. He had already tasted his spearmint one so he opted for the most unusual flavour from the list the chemist recited to him.

"I'll have a liquorice one please," he beamed back, reaching out with his brass thruppenny bit.

Tommy happily pocketed his change and left for the station, brandishing his stick lolly and sucking at the base before the melting ice could drip on his uniform. The stroll to reach the platform passed blissfully as he rolled the lolly round in his mouth, alternately sucking and biting until it was reduced to a thin sliver clinging to the wooden stem. By now his tongue and lips were a vivid blue-black, but Tommy didn't care at all. There was no one he knew to tease him about it.

When he reached the station platform the happy memory of the lolly was fading and a cloud of loneliness descended about the forlorn figure. A shudder passed through his shoulders as he looked about and noted that all the other passengers were adults. Glancing up at the large station clock, he noticed that the minute hand had just crept past the Roman numeral IV.

Another ten minutes before the train even arrives! he thought gloomily. By the time I get home and have my tea the night will be nearly gone – and I've still got some English homework to do for tomorrow.

Reaching into his pockets once again, he recovered his penny change from the chemist's. There were two other penny coins in his other pocket. He could at least do something about his hunger pains that had returned after the effect of the lolly had worn off. Luckily the station buffet was still open for business. A cheery warmth met him as he entered the bright interior. Shuffling up to the counter, he asked for a packet of crisps.

Stepping outside once more, he tore open the bag and grabbed several pieces of his favourite flavoured Rishy crisps. Cheese crisps! Lovely thick ones laced with a strong cheesy coating. The crumbs stuck to his lips as well as his fingers, recreating a thirst which had been slaked by the liquorice lolly. Licking the last remnants from his person, Tommy wiped his sleeve across his mouth.

Thankfully the train steamed in slightly early. Tommy followed a large lady and two young men into a non-corridor compartment. He was able to curl up into a corner seat, clutching his school bag. Peering out through the grime-caked window he saw a haunted figure looking back at him. Averting his eyes from his dejected reflection, he looked up at the fitful twilight sky with purple clouds racing across his view.

Just as his mind began to dwell on home and the promise of a hot meal and sympathy, the world suddenly turned black. Of course, it was the long tunnel out of Blackburn station! Chiding himself for forgetting this in his dark despair, Tommy poked his tongue out at the two chaps sitting opposite him. He only just retracted it in time as the evening murk replaced the depths of the tunnel night.

That silly interlude seemed to revive Tommy's spirits, especially as the plump lady at the other end of his seat gave him a radiant smile. Did she know what he had just done under cover of darkness?

Accrington hove into view, meaning a five minute wait here as the connecting line from Manchester brought its own train to meet Tommy's for an exchange of passengers.

Then it was onward again, past the halts of Huncoat and Hapton, the marshalling yards of Rosegrove and then Burnley Central station. At last, after a brief pause at Brierfield, the train finally lumbered into Nelson with a screech of brakes.

Tired as he was by now, Tommy nevertheless strove to walk up the rise of Hibson Road with a firm tread. After five minutes of leg-cramping effort, he was able to drag himself up the short flight of steps leading to the front door, twist the handle and push on into the hallway.

"Where on earth have you been?" was the first response from the bosom of his family.

Oh well, no point in trying to hide the truth, thought Tommy resignedly, then aloud, "Er, I got put in detention."

"What on earth for?"

What's earth got to do with it? (again to himself) before admitting, "I didn't get good enough marks in maths and English." Well, not strictly true – but he couldn't admit to being cheeky to his teacher, could he?

"English and Maths are the most important subjects. You've got to do better than that, Tommy," was the verdict from Dad.

Mum, being more understanding of a young chap's problems, proffered him a cup of tea and informed him that tea would be ready soon. This seemed to end any further speculation on the problem, though Tommy couldn't help notice the sly smirk from Shirley that spoke volumes.

There would be many more such frustrating home-comings over the winter months. If it wasn't detention or late trains, admittedly quite rare, there was the inexorable drawing in of the long nights. By the time that tea had been taken and homework completed, there was simply no daylight left for outdoor companionship.

So it was that Tommy felt himself drifting further and further away from the friendships of his childhood. His erstwhile mates didn't have any homework to speak of, and not only that, they were home from school by half past four.

It was good old Eric who, to some extent, came to the rescue. Eric was proving to be a very good and dependable pal to Tommy. He didn't see anything untoward in the fact that Tommy's schooling was different from the norm for the neighbourhood, or that it should be a source of discord.

It was Eric who brought up the subject of the Scouts.

"There's a new Scout troop starting up in the Methodist Church Hall. Do you fancy joining?" he asked.

"Er, I don't really know. What do you have to do?" was Tommy's first response.

"Well, you have to wear the uniform and learn some rules and laws. You have to go to the meetings regularly and take part in the activities."

"I don't know. I've got my homework to do every night…"

"Go on, it'll be good fun. After a while, you get to go on camps with the Scoutmasters and the others."

Tommy didn't want to lose his one good friend so he agreed to give it a try. At least the meetings were on Thursday nights when he didn't have as much homework and some of this could be delayed until the weekend.

Somewhat to Tommy's relief, his parents thought it was a great idea for him to join the troop. They took him to the shop and gladly kitted him out with the khaki uniform. They even bought him a knife and sheath which strapped to the belt of his shorts.

Eric called for him at 6.15. Together they strolled down to the Methodist Hall feeling slightly self-conscious in their pristine kit. At least it was now dark at this time in the evening. They met up with one or two familiar faces at the door. Pushing into the dusty interior, they ascended the short flight of stairs and entered the long, narrow hall.

There were windows set high on the walls (just like his junior school), a worn and scrubbed bare wooden floor and two doors at the far end which led to a small washroom and a janitor's cupboard.

The Scoutmaster was smartly turned out in a larger version of their own uniform, save that his was bristling with cloth badges and a couple of enamel ones. He was quite tall, bespectacled and lean. His second-in-command, by contrast, was of much thicker and squatter build, more of the rugged outdoor type one would associate with Scouting. He was Mr Garbutt, while his superior was called Mr Frankland.

The new recruits, as well as the older hands who had joined all of two weeks ago, were told to squat on the floor in a semicircle. There they were addressed by their leader, who informed them what a great calling it was to be a Scout, to follow in the footsteps of Lord Baden-Powell and to take on the responsibility of membership. This entailed not only helping one's fellow man but being at the behest of one's Queen and country, ready to serve them in time of need.

Suitably impressed, not to say chastened, the group of boys repeated the words of the Scouting Law as recited to them by Mr Garbutt. They were then allowed to engage in a series of games involving healthy exercise and teamwork.

Finally, they were brought back together for prayers and a reminder to make sure that they came in good time for the next meeting.

As they spilled out into the chill night air, Eric said, "Well, did you like it?"

"Yeah, it was good fun," replied Tommy truthfully.

They strode out for home feeling quite pleased with themselves, even if their knees were feeling the draught.

Parting at the corner of Bradshaw and Camden Street, they muttered their farewells. Tommy skipped down the street and bounced into his backyard, feeling that perhaps he could still have some fun and friends after all.

The First Year

J oining the Scouts and finding a good mate in Eric weren't
the only new experiences that Tommy would enjoy that
year.

There was not least the new travel companion who
shared the compartment with the boys on their morning
journey. Pauline appeared one day, boarding at Brierfield
and journeying to Accrington. She must have been travelling the same route for some time. One day she shared their
compartment. This became a regular thing and soon the
confident Pauline began to chat at length with the three
boys.

She was good-looking, admitted Tommy, even if she did
seem a little old in her ways. Whatever, Pauline gradually
became more friendly in a way that was a pleasant surprise
to Tommy. Mind you, in his experience, girls had always
seemed more confident in the company of boys than he had
ever felt with them. She seemed perfectly at home chatting
to the three of them and she didn't display any sign of
discomfort or shyness at the fact that she was the only girl in
their company.

Tommy began to look forward to the mornings when
Pauline would grace them with her company. Of course,
she was only being matey and passing the time, and there
was only one of her compared to three of them. Nevertheless, he gradually grew very fond of her.

They never saw her on the journey home. Perhaps she
caught a different train from Accrington in the evenings.

One morning John was ill. Pauline shared the compartment with Frank and Tommy. This slightly increased

intimacy gave her the opportunity she needed. Before the boys realised it, Pauline had persuaded them to let her comb their hair.

How she revelled in this new departure. The two boys took it in turns to sit meekly while she borrowed their combs and busied herself shaping and playing with their locks. It was a very pleasant experience and they were willing and compliant subjects.

They were to share such intimacy with Pauline on several more occasions. In fact they went out of their way to devise strategies for ensuring that she would be able to share the compartment in private with the two of them.

Alas, before their companionship could develop further, Pauline informed them one morning that she and her family were moving house. Not only that, they were going to live in the Midlands and she would also be leaving the school.

Tommy thought wistfully that she was the second girl that he had begun to grow rather fond of, and one who would also drift out of his life. It wasn't as if she was his special friend anyway. He had had to share her company with Frank.

The sharp coldness of new year winter bore through the gloom of the short days. Snowball fights became a regular feature of the walks to school and the impatient minutes spent waiting on the station platforms. There was one particular occasion when a flurry of wind-driven snow covered the platform at Nelson Station as the commuters and pupils awaited their transport. Needing no further encouragement, the boys gleefully scooped up handfuls of the still fresh, damp snow and moulded it in to icy balls. When the train came huffing in to collect its cargo, they hurled their misshapen bombs at the steaming funnel and then at the carriage windows as they glided past.

More than one outward peering face reared back in surprise as a blob of slush thudded against the window, only to trickle down in a dying smear of melt water. The indignant voice and shaking fist of a porter sent the boys scurrying to board the train and lose themselves along the corridors before he could exact retribution.

Breathing heavily and convulsed with laughter, they collapsed in an empty compartment. The shrill whistle of the flag-wielding guard was shortly followed by a sharp jerk as the carriage responded to the first tug of the departing locomotive.

This was the point at which John decided to get rid of the rapidly melting ball of icy snow that he had clung on to. He chose the back of Tommy's neck.

"Aaargh! You swine!" roared Tommy as the contents slithered down the back of his collar.

Frank's hoarse laughter was drowned in the noise of the wrestling match between Tommy and John. This ended when the pair of them rolled onto the floor of the compartment and were met by a blast of dusty hot air from the under-seat heating. Strangely, this cooled their ardour sufficiently for them to clamber into their seats and begin rearranging their dishevelled attire.

"You wait till we get off at Blackburn," threatened Tommy.

This was greeted with a contemptuous smirk and gesture from John. By the time they hove into the platform at Blackburn all was of course forgotten, if not forgiven.

There was a brief flurry of white missiles exchanged between the St Mary's lads and those of QEGS before they separated to board their respective buses.

That particular winter contained several particular memories. There was the drama of the bus crash when a double-decker slithered down East Park Road and out on to the main road at the junction, there to collide with a large lorry feeling its way down towards the centre. After the initial shock at the splintering crunch, the boys tumbled off the bus to briefly gawp at the damage before making their way on foot to the station.

Then there was the fun of the football match played on a snow-bound school field. Mr Kennedy, the maths teacher, doubling up as games master decided that it was not too bad to prevent the boys getting their fresh air. Thus they emerged from the pavilion shivering onto a field ankle deep in a fresh coating of white.

It turned out that his decision was a sound one as the eighteen boys involved soon warmed to the occasion. They laughed heartily at their own efforts to propel the football, resulting in immediate opponents being covered in a spray of snowflakes. With reddening faces and dripping noses they cavorted about in a parody of a football game before retiring dripping wet and with plastered hair back to the changing room.

Winter gave way to spring and the increasingly warm evenings. When these became light enough to permit outdoor play there was an extra urgency to complete the set homework for the night in order to allow for some time to be spent with one's best mates, even if their education had taken a very different path for the past year.

So it became possible for Tommy to renew and even strengthen his bond with Eric. The two boys shared common interests. They were both basically shy and modest creatures, more comfortable in their own shared company than in the larger grouping of any local gang. Neither of them felt drawn to the antics of the group of boys who dwelled upon the very word of the brash and ebullient Brian.

Tommy was to spend many a happy weekend afternoon, and even weekday evening when it became lighter and when homework wasn't too demanding, in Eric's company.

If the weather was inclement, they would adjourn to Eric's parlour. Eric had a Subbuteo set. Not only that, he had had the baize pitch fastened to a sheet of plywood. This meant, of course, that matches could be played on an immaculate surface devoid of wrinkles or kinks.

Many a happy wet afternoon was spent by the two of them competing in FA Cups and World Cup tournaments. Lists of competing teams were drawn up, lots were cast and play engaged until one of them emerged victorious.

Close of play was usually followed by portions of ice cream and tinned blackcurrants lovingly served up by Eric's mum. On selected evenings, this was concluded with a session round the television. The Calvert's had still not succumbed to the fashion of owning a television set. It was thus a great treat for Tommy to be able to watch episodes of Popeye cartoons and even the "I Love Lucy Show", though he obviously preferred the former.

The friendship between Eric and Tommy began to lose its exclusivity and innocence. This development started when they joined the rest of the lads for the larger gatherings outside the chip shop on Beaufort Street. Those with spare cash would purchase a bag of chips or a bottle of Tizer. That, however, was not the main purpose of the meeting. It was to socialise, to mix and exchange patter, to brag and boast about exploits.

Inevitably, such groupings became of mixed gender. Whilst the boys still considerably outnumbered the girls there was much rivalry for affection but not much in the way of actual liaison. That situation altered, though, when it became clear that two particular girls were kindred spirits to Eric and Tommy.

Wendy was the more vivacious. All the boys fancied her. Her companion, Doreen, though not as pretty, was nevertheless very friendly and cheerful in an endearing way.

It must have been Eric who made the first approach. Tommy would never have done so. It seemed that the girls had agreed to meet the two of them on Saturday morning.

What for? thought Tommy to himself and then aloud to Eric: "What are we going to do?"

Eric, though equally inexperienced, didn't seem to be panicked by the thought.

As it turned out, the lads met at ten o'clock and sauntered across to the field by the allotments. Wendy and Doreen arrived shortly afterwards. Eric had brought a tennis ball. Before Tommy realised what was happening, the four of them were engaged in a game of catch. The boys threw the ball to each other while the girls attempted to intercept the pass. When the ball changed hands and the boys tried to thwart the girls, Tommy became engrossed in the activity.

It took some time before the hidden agenda dawned on Tommy, unused as he was to such mixed occupation. At first, he was engrossed with the aim of keeping the ball between himself and Eric. Soon, however, he found himself in situations where he had to physically compete with Doreen for possession of the ball. On such occasions he at first endeavoured to wrest the ball away from her. Then his politeness and sense of chivalry began to intrude. He held back just a little to allow Doreen a better chance to get the ball.

Was this merely good manners or was some other instinct at work? Doreen knew what was going on. She took advantage in the beginning and grasped the ball whenever she could. Then she began to hold back. She would wait until Tommy had the ball and then vigorously try to wrestle it away from him in a most unladylike fashion. The same scenario was enacted between Eric and Wendy.

The games concluded without any further ritual. Tired and happy, the four of them would trudge homeward, each with a feeling of inner warmth and bliss. Whenever the four of them met up with the rest of the local youth, their time together was never mentioned. It was only a friendship and it was never to become anything more, but it was somehow special enough not to risk being tainted by revealing its existence to everyone else.

Alas, Tommy's hours at home were increasingly filled by his schoolwork commitments. Thus he was only able to catch up on the local scene at weekends and therefore he became gradually but inexorably more distanced from his peers. He had his school chums, of course, but their company was limited to the train journeys or free time during the school day. This would become the pattern for Tommy's social development – shared company during the daytime, isolation in the evenings.

The day arrived when the Calvert family joined the increasing number of local residents who had made a lifestyle change. They acquired a television set. It was a table-top model, black and white of course. It was quite large – a wooden cabinet with a grey curved screen and a row of control buttons along the bottom. There was the on/off switch, volume control, vertical and horizontal holds and a brightness switch. It was rented by the month from the electrical shop in town.

Dad had it mounted on a large occasional table in the corner of the sitting room, on the opposite side to the gramophone player which occupied the recess to the right of the fireplace.

Although it could receive programmes from both the BBC and ITV channel, it was only switched on for the occasional programme of general family interest. At other times the radio or gramophone continued to provide any necessary amusement. What the television did achieve, though, was to impede Tommy's educational progress. It could be argued that it broadened the horizon of his experience by bringing the world beyond East Lancashire within his ken. It was most certainly the case that it proved to be a powerful distraction.

Unable to bear being out of the room whenever the set was switched on, Tommy took to doing his homework at the dining table. Seated thus behind the rest of his family, he pored over his books. Frequent and ever lengthening glances would be made at the screen. Such constant sparring between homework and TV programme inevitably led to errors in his work or to poor quality writing. It would even lead to homework being incomplete, though Tommy would never admit this to his mum and dad.

The knock-on effect of this was that homework was often completed on the train the following morning. Not only was this an unsatisfactory environment but it also somewhat curtailed his social life. As well as being unable to fully join in with the larking about that the boys got up to en route, it gained him rather unfairly and inaccurately the label of swot. Not that he was the only one who made up for lack of concentration the previous evening. Several of the boys began to use their bonus travelling time to complete assignments.

It became an acquired skill to handwrite answers in exercise books that were resting on satchels balanced on the knees.

This practise was fraught with danger. There was the ever present threat of some prankster knocking away the supporting school bag or nudging an elbow. A slight rocking of the train on uneven track could cause a pen nib to lurch across the page. Small wonder that several exercise books began to bear the red ink critique of a master's comment to the effect that penmanship appeared to be a dying art among the youth of today.

Even worse was the prospect of having to complete an exercise on the bus during the final run up to school, with its packed bodies and swaying, standing passengers.

Needless to say, some homeworks remained incomplete

upon being handed in. This had a tendency to lead to the occasional detention or even caning.

The teachers, both lay and religious, were not averse to resorting to the instruments of correction on those occasions when they deemed it necessary. Such occasions seemed to crop up quite frequently, suggesting that the leather straps and canes were not quite regarded as the final and unavoidable resort.

Physical chastisements became the norm not just for sloppy work but especially for transgressions of behaviour. While being strapped for producing poor work could be a source of shame, that for misbehaviour was sometimes a means of raising esteem and attracting admiration from one's peers. The strap, and sometimes the cane, made more than a casual acquaintance with Tommy – or at least with the palms of his hands.

More Experience

Father Short was very inappropriately named. Either the good Lord was having a laugh or the family genes went astray somewhere along the line. He stood a towering six feet two inches with plenty of lateral bulk as well. He was knocking on a bit and was even a little round shouldered, so as a young priest he must have cut a formidable figure. He was well known to pupils of all ages for he ran the tuck shop. This extremely popular facility was a scene of frantic activity at the morning break when near starving boys sought to appease their hunger pangs. It would have been some three hours since the longest travelling members of the school population had partaken of their breakfasts.

Father Short made great capital of this. He stocked boxes of sweet and filling confections – toffee and caramel bars and chocolate – and he didn't charge overly excessive prices. Eagerly queuing pupils would be greeted with the inevitable, "And what can I do you for?" from the voice above as he held out his palm for their pennies.

Tommy was a regular customer and usually purchased a bar of Highland Toffee or MacKay's Devon Toffee – the latter having the added luxury of a chocolate coating around the extremely hard confection. The contents would eventually succumb to the oral juices and vigorous chewing that his mouth could inflict upon them.

No one, at least in the lower school, seemed to know precisely what function Father Short performed within the staff team – apart, that is, from his retail duties.

They were left in no doubt about one part of his role: that of slave master. One of the playgrounds consisted of a cinder surface which was all right for football games until anyone was foolish enough to lose his balance. Frequent departures from the pitch became a necessary part of most games. Victims would repair to the toilets to bathe badly grazed knees and remove the bulk of the imbedded grit. Wise pupils would roll up the tops of their socks to cover the knees. These were the short trouser wearers, of whom Tommy was one. The sophisticates who sported long trousers found that decreased wounding to the knees was replaced by increased damage to the trouser, and this could not be sponged away.

As to the unsuitability of the cinder surface for vigorous youthful play, the thoughtful Father Short had plans. He had managed to secure sufficient funds from the college to resurface the yard, but only if he could save on the labour. Thus it was that a local builder's suppliers had dropped off a large quantity of concrete flagstones. These were left propped against the red brick wall of the classroom block.

Further progress on the project was left to the capability and ingenuity of the enterprising Father Short. Not one to shirk strenuous physical labour, he set about raking and levelling the cinder surface as best he could. When this task was done, it was a simple matter to recruit willing hands to help him complete the work.

The first that the unsuspecting pupils became aware of their plight was when a huge frocked figure loomed in to view around the corner of the yard. It was the turn of an unfortunate group of lads which included Tommy and Frank. Before their surprise could manifest itself in an instinct for flight, the huge beckoning finger of Father Short demanded their subservience.

When the boys reluctantly followed his footsteps, cursing their ill fortune at losing the freedom of their play time, they saw to their horror the fate that awaited them.

It was made abundantly clear that they were expected to lift and haul the flagstones in to place so that their slave master could set them in position on the cinder bed. Each grasping a corner of the flagstone, the first batch of four prisoners lifted and staggered with their load across to the waiting priest.

Two successful such trips took place. With the third flag, the boys valiantly struggled across the yard with aching arms. Just as they were about to gently lower the stone to the ground, one of the four (it was neither Tommy nor Frank) found that his grip was no longer up to the task. As the unfortunate lad's fingers slid away from the corner of the flagstone, it dropped heavily to the ground. Luckily for him and the others, they were able to jump out of the way to avoid crushed toes. Unluckily, the flagstone did not escape injury. As it hit the ground at an awkward angle, a large piece broke off from the corner where the hapless boy had let go.

The boys were still breathing heavily after their narrow brush with misfortune when Father Short instructed one of them to fetch the strap from the staff room. They were still puzzling over this request when the errand boy returned. Their curiosity was soon dispelled as they were each told to offer their palms in submission. The angry cleric extracted vengeance for the destruction of his precious property by administering a hearty wallop to the outstretched hands of all four of them.

It was the only time that Tommy was caught in this cruel situation. From then on, he and his friends were most careful about their choice of play site in order not to be surprised by a sudden visit from the sadistic labourer.

The sharp lesson that Tommy had learned about discipline and chastisement at St Mary's prepared him for future brushes with authority. On the whole, the not infrequent punishments were deserved, which is more than could be said for Father Short's version of justice.

In point of fact, Tommy grew to prefer the instant retribution of corporal punishment to the indignity and shame of detention and bad report cards. At least there was no way that the strappings would become known to his parents. He certainly wouldn't tell them if the school kept their counsel. That, of course, was the whole point of the strapping; it was instant, painful and soon forgotten, at least by the masters, even if it took some hand wringing, blowing cheeks and cold water dunking on the part of the victim.

Most of the strappings were administered for behavioural reasons. Tommy sometimes groaned at his misfortune at (some would say propensity for) being caught in flagrante of school codes of behaviour.

Did he deserve to be strapped just for larking about in the toilets at break time, or for running down the corridor in continuation of a game of tig after the bell? What about the time he knocked at the staff room door and enquired as to the whereabouts of a member of staff who had asked him to report? The fact that he had inadvertently asked, "Is Mr Otto in?" instead of asking for the language master, Mr Whiteoak. Well, he and everyone else had long been in the habit of calling their dear Latin teacher by his universal nickname. It had simply slipped out.

It was almost a welcome change to receive a novel form of beating. When Tommy and Steve were deemed to have been impertinent to the craftwork teacher, Miss Leaver, the science master (one "Beaky" Rigby) extracted revenge with a few hefty swipes of a slipper to their rear ends. He seemed to take it personally. Well, it was rumoured among the boys that he had a soft spot for her.

It would be a mistake to assume that such experiences made Tommy's life unpleasant or to think that St Mary's was an uncaring and sadistic institution. The boys were, after all, like growing lads everywhere; a spirited and lively collection who were in need of firm guidance in order that their energies be channelled in useful and formative ways. Goodness knows, there were times when the boot was on the other foot. They could be cruel in their treatment of any member of staff who was neither sufficiently forceful or blessed with a sense of humour that could gain their respect and loyalty.

Take poor Mr Baxenden, for instance. This wretched member of staff joined the modern languages department in Tommy's third year. Now, Tommy quite liked French lessons. This was due to the fact that he had gained very high marks in the subject in his first year. Furthermore, during his second year he was accorded great praise by the not unattractive Miss Forbes.

During one lesson which involved the boys being asked to count in French and recite simple sentences, she had remarked to the whole class (and much to Tommy's embarrassment and secret pride) after his spoken efforts, "He sounds just like a little French boy!"

Compared to the general utterings of the rest of the class in undisguised Lanky-twang French, this was only a moderate achievement. Still, if it gave Miss Forbes pleasure, that was good enough for Tommy.

Anyway, back to the experiences of Mr Baxenden. It was a shame really. Not for Mr B, who should have been up to the task, but for Tommy. He had warmed to the task of mastering the rudiments of a foreign language. Such enthusiasm was to take a back seat to the ever popular sport of teacher baiting.

There were not many occasions when the boys could dare to try to get one over a member of staff, not with the ever present threat of the strap or detention. Besides, most of the teachers were well capable of meeting fire with fire. Not so Mr Baxenden.

Where on earth had this guy been trained? From what planet had he landed? The boys wasted little time on such surmising. Ever willing to exploit any weakness, they saw a gilt-edged opportunity to indulge in great fun to lighten up the day's drudgery. Baxenden was of the old school. That is to say, he attempted to deliver his lessons from the desk. With head buried in his textbook and prepared notes, he droned on to the class. Occasionally he would look up to peer at them through his thick lenses, but rarely made eye contact with any pupil.

Boys began to whisper, none too quietly, among themselves. Cottoning on to the fact that they weren't pulled up for this, they began to indulge in further distracting activities. If challenged by Mr Baxenden, they would feign innocence and make great play of eliciting his sympathy. No stern punishments were forthcoming.

Thus emboldened, one or two boys began to leave their seats whenever the teacher's back was turned. If he began to write on the blackboard, they would indulge in a silent form of musical chairs.

It wasn't long before some bright spark hit upon the idea of pre-empting the evening's homework. While a couple of boys occupied Mr Baxenden's attention by coming out to his desk to ask for help or to have work marked, one member of the class would sneak behind the desk. Looking over his shoulder, he would then read the notes which contained the set homework.

On returning to his desk, the appointed pupil would pass round the acquired details of the set work to the rest of the class. Thus informed, everyone then set about completing the evening's homework during the lesson. Not content with such felony, the boys decided to extract maximum humour from the situation.

Just before the bell, Mr Baxenden would begin to announce the task: "For homework tonight, I want you to do—"

Some bright spark would then reply, "—Page 51, exercises a, b and c."

"How… how do you know?" spluttered Mr B.

"Oh, just a lucky guess, sir!" was the cheerful reply.

This happy situation continued until the time when one idiot took things too far. He handed in his book for marking at the end of the same lesson in which the homework had just been set. Even Baxenden smelled a rat. No strappings were forthcoming. He was probably too ashamed to admit his naivety.

After that, the boys contented themselves with humiliating their French teacher in even more outrageous fashion. It became common practise to purloin a piece of chalk and to write various jibes and insults on his academic gown. How he explained away such graffiti when he retired to the staff room is anyone's guess.

Sadly, for those pupils who appreciated the chance to actually extract humour from their lessons, Baxenden was a one-off – at least as far as St Mary's was concerned. As for the rest of the teaching staff, the strap and detention were administered as if they were an intrinsic part of the required syllabus.

There were teachers who had a streak of humour and some understanding of the spirit of their charges. These tended to be tolerant of the more harmless if silly pranks and japes of the boys. Thankfully, among the ranks of these enlightened tutors was the Headmaster, Father Grey.

The pupils respected these staff. They didn't seek indulgence or kindness from them. Rather, they would have regarded such characteristics as weaknesses to be exploited. No, they could accept the occasional chastisement from them in the knowledge that grudges would not be held. If errant behaviour met its reward, then this was a fair cop.

An Outing

Tommy rarely bothered to relate any of his school experiences to his local playmates. After all, his was an educational world quite removed from that enjoyed by them. They had less academically trained but by all accounts more worldly-wise and with-it teachers; mentors who knew that they were rearing a body of pupils who would need to acquire the life skills and common sense to enable them to cope in the harsh world of adult employment that would await them soon after they reached the ripe age of sixteen.

Gradually, Tommy was drifting further away from the friendships of his early childhood. This wasn't because of any snobbishness on his part, but was simply down to the reality that homework commitments precluded companionship on most evenings. His erstwhile mates, by comparison, were unrestricted by any such demands. Indeed, they seemed to be largely blissfully unaware of school work after hours. Four o'clock for them meant a release from the school regime until the next day. Not so with Tommy.

The welcome distraction of the television set, which seemed to be switched on for an increasing amount of time in the evenings, only served to increase Tommy's burden. An evening's homework task that once would have taken perhaps a half-hour to finish managed to stretch in to an hour and a half or more. For all the extra time spent, the quality of the completed work would not increase much, if at all.

Increasingly, any companionship that Tommy enjoyed came from the company of his fellow travellers. After all, he spent about one and a half hours each school day sharing a train seat with them. Added to that was the waiting time and the minutes spent on the bus up to school or the walk back down to town. Little wonder, then, that he felt he had more in common with his secondary school companions than his street pals.

The sad thing was that his railway company ended each time the train ground to a halt at the stations en route and a few pals spilled out onto the platform. At Nelson, the terminus as far as Tommy was concerned, farewells were exchanged as he and his school mates emerged from the station complex onto the concourse and car park.

Tommy shared part of the journey up Hibson Road with Frank before the latter muttered goodbye and headed towards Wadeshouse Road and home.

The world that Tommy now lived in was lopsided in that it was an all-male environment. Only boys of course attended St Mary's, so unlike the friends of former days, he didn't experience mixed company during school hours.

There were the girls from the Notre Dame Convent, of course. These numbered seven or eight in total, three of whom travelled most of the way on Tommy's train, but they tended to keep themselves to themselves. Dressed in their green uniforms with matching hats, replaced by straw "boaters" in the summer, they too clung to each other for moral support and only cast covert glances to the boys from St Mary's or QEGS. It was probably because they attended an all-girls' school and the boys were similarly in all-male company that they did not readily mix.

Tommy knew from his companions the names of the three girls who shared their journey. There was Jean, the slim, quite tall and rather snooty one. Actually she reminded Tommy of his own older sister. Katherine was quite different in build. She was pleasantly plump with a cheery face but just the hint of a double chin, emphasised by the strap of her bonnet, which sunk into it. She lived in Burnley. Finally there was Hazel from Brierfield. With bright auburn hair and a fetching sprinkling of freckles she was strikingly the prettiest of the threesome. She had an elfin face which, when meeting a boy's gaze along with her sparkling blue eyes, caused hearts to miss a beat. Many a young lad's thoughts became distracted and resolve turned to nothing when confronted by her smile.

Several of the bolder boys attempted without much success to gain her favour. One day they noted with great frustration that she seemed to be of close acquaintance with a rather rough and ordinary looking lad who had come to meet her as she alighted from the train.

Katherine, Tommy noticed, favoured him on more than one occasion with a look of interest. At these times he was prone to averting his gaze out of shyness. He didn't dare let it show in front of the boys that he felt encouraged and flattered by her warmth. He genuinely liked her, but how could he reciprocate his feelings sufficiently? Besides, she got off the train before him and there was no opportunity to even be in her vicinity without the company of the other boys and girls. Thus such frustrating lack of meaningful communication dragged on for months. The boys never shared a compartment with the girls so any interchanges were limited to the minutes spent on the station platform awaiting the arrival of the homeward-bound train.

In the spring Tommy was to experience more feelings of uncertainty with regard to the fairer sex. The Scout meetings resumed after the Christmas break and these were transferred to the vacant school rooms attached to the Methodist parish. There had been changes of personnel in the adult Scout leaders and this resulted in a rather lax regime. Many a time the boys arrived in the main hall only to find that they had to wait for their Scoutmaster and his assistant.

Things livened up when a Girl Guide unit was set up. The Guides met on the same night, presumably because this was when the suite of rooms was more easily available. The Guides met in the smaller room attached to the main hall.

One evening when the boys were awaiting their tardy leader as usual, they heard the sound of the girls being drilled next door. Brian was the first to have the idea of spying on them. He climbed up on a desk until he could see through the window set high up in the partition. He was soon joined by several other eager faces who gazed in rapture at the girls practising formation marching.

It wasn't long before their sniggering and muffled catcalls came to the attention of the Guide leader. That was the end of that particular entertainment. The experience left Tommy and one or two others wondering why they didn't all meet together. But that would never have been allowed by the Guide mistress, even if the laid-back Scoutmaster had agreed to the merger.

There was some good news regarding the Scout patrol's activities. All those who passed the Tenderfoot stage would be allowed to go camping for the weekend at Whitsuntide. This led to a flurry of effort and concentration on the part of the troop. The Scout Law was memorised, knots were practised and badges entered for. All this took a toll on Tommy's homework commitments and caused him to lapse from time to time, thus leading to the inevitable detention.

It was all worthwhile when he was allowed, along with most of the patrol, to join the camping expedition. In fact, of his immediate pals, only Ronnie was not going and that had more to do with his reluctance to be parted from the bosom of home to rough it with the others.

As the May days dragged on towards the camping deadline, Tommy became increasingly excited. He polished his Scout knife, read his handbook, wrote out his equipment list and studied the Ordnance Survey map. At last, the time arrived.

Tommy spent a sleepless night tossing and turning in his bed and wondering how he would cope with the primitive life, albeit for only two days. Like the rest of the boys, he had never been away from home and family for twenty-four hours.

The boys were to meet up with one another and with their Scoutmasters at the town centre bus stop. They duly gathered, engaged in animated chatter, and inevitably waited for their leader, who arrived in the nick of time. Boarding the single-decker bus, they shuffled into their seats after swinging their backpacks onto the floor by their feet.

"Single to Blacko," they echoed in turn as the thin and rather bony conductor swayed down the aisle with palm outstretched for their coppers. They were halfway to Barrowford by the time the conductor had wound out separate tickets for each of them as they proffered their fares.

The bus soon ground up the hill through the long climb past the terraced cottages. It stopped outside the small village shop and post office. This was their stop. Hurriedly they squeezed and pushed to the front door to be sure of dismounting before the bus set off again towards Gisburn.

While the eager but disorganised Scout leaders attempted to muster their charges into an organised patrol for the final march to their intended campsite, several members of the troop led by Brian sloped off to the shop to purchase last-minute survival rations. These included boxes of matches and, for one boy who had not managed to pack his in secret, a pack of ten cigarettes. Apparently he had managed to convince the elderly lady behind the counter that they were for his Scoutmaster.

Thus armed and sufficiently provisioned to survive a weekend under the stars and away from home comforts and TV, the party set out jauntily down the path that ran alongside the dry stone wall skirting the meadow. This plunged down towards the valley bottom.

They were soon hidden from view of the main road and from a sighting of Blacko Tower behind them. To compensate, they had a splendid sighting of the big end of Pendle Hill away across the far side of the valley.

Near the bottom of the field, Mr Garbutt halted the group and pointed them towards a stile set in the wall. This consisted of two projecting stones which led up to a gap in the coping and over to another matching pair of stones on the opposite side.

Clambering one at a time with trailing rucksacks buffeting the wall, the boys climbed and then jumped into the adjacent field. A well worn path led down towards a trickle of a stream. The party halted by a little bluff a few yards up from the water. This was fairly level – at least level enough to enable them to pitch tents.

The boys divided roughly in to four groups and were then given the task of erecting the canvas homes that would each sleep between three and four. It was necessary for the Scout leaders to intervene and assist each group at some stage, but eventually they managed the task.

The boys were made to lay out their belongings and prepare their beds before any other activity could be contemplated. Firewood was then gathered to supplement the stock brought with them and the gas stoves held by the adults. Stones had to be prised from outcrops or the stream bed to make fire surrounds.

At last they were allowed to explore their environment with a firm reminder to respect the countryside and the lives of the wild creatures and local farmers. The stream was to be their bathroom for pre-meal ablutions. When the boys had all suitably cleansed themselves they were mustered around the campfires to cook and partake of their evening meal.

After much fussing with building and stoking fires,

erecting cooking frames and filling pots, they hunkered down to tend to the boiling and frying process. Eyes streamed with tears as the acrid, stinging smoke wafted over those who were in close attendance. Fingers became streaked and smudged as they prodded sticks in the fire rendering their earlier efforts at hand washing pointless.

Eventually, some semblance of a meal found its way onto the metal plates of each boy and adult. The contents were swiftly devoured.

"Nothing like fresh air to give you an appetite!" declared the Scoutmaster unnecessarily.

The boys decided that their appetites would not be assuaged until they had had a chance to consume their caches of sweets and chocolate.

An impromptu game of football followed the domestic chores. This was soon abandoned as they discovered that an undulating meadow complete with tufts of thistles and animal waste products did not make for a suitable playing surface.

There was the required gathering round the remnants of the campfire while the wise elders held an open-air lesson in Scout lore followed by tales and miming games. The boys were encouraged to perform their pre-sleep toilet and to retire to their separate tents for the night.

Out came comics, books and torches for the indoor pastimes. The Scoutmasters made a final round of the tents to check up on their charges before retiring themselves. After this inspection, carefully stashed cigarettes and matches made a miraculous appearance in more than one tent.

Tommy was sharing with Eric, Dave and Neil. It was Eric who first lit up and puffed away with the expertise of someone who was familiar with the process involved. He introduced Neil, who claimed that he had smoked before, to the business of lighting and smoking his own. Then it was Tommy's turn to be loaned Eric's cigarette for an exploratory puff. He filled his mouth with smoke, then coughed and spluttered as he breathed out. This amused the others so much they asked for a repeat performance.

"Eurrgh!" he gasped after a second attempt, "Why do you bother?"

"Don't you like it?" grinned Eric, who had gone down a little in Tommy's estimation.

The boys began one by one to slip into their sleeping bags. Propped up on their elbows, they chattered, laughed and whispered for some time. Torches were finally extinguished after much rustling of paper, giggling and catcalling, and tired bodies finally succumbed to slumber.

Tommy was roused from sleep by Dave treading all over his prone form and declaring that he urgently needed to go for a wee. And now the whole business of washing, preparing fires and gathering supplies began again. In fact, it resembled in a primitive way the daily chores of a household, but this irony was lost on the boys, who were taking part in an adventure not unlike those undertaken by their screen heroes.

Eric went off with Tommy to collect more wood for the fire. Being unable to find sufficient windfall branches for their needs, Eric introduced Tommy to a camper's trick. He instructed him to use an axe to chop off a sturdy side branch from a sapling. When Tommy had managed this, Eric scooped up some mud from the bank of the stream and smeared it on the bare stem from which the branch had been hacked.

"This is to disguise it so that no one can see the fresh wood where you chopped it off," he loftily informed Tommy.

This led Tommy to the conclusion that what they had just done was somehow wrong, either in the eyes of the Scoutmaster or the farmer, or possibly both.

They managed to return unscathed to camp and dispose

of the evidence in the flames before any accusing eyes could cause awkward questions to be asked.

All too soon it seemed to be time to strike camp and head for home. Tents and belongings were wrapped up with rather less care than when the boys had set out. A stiff climb back up the meadow led them to the bus shelter and thence a short ride back to the bosom of their families.

Alas, if the boys had but realised it at the time, such adventures were to succumb to the inevitable march towards adulthood upon which they were all engaged, though blissfully unaware of the consequences.

Changing World

S ummer gave way to a damp, breezy autumn. The steam trains had finally all but given way some time ago to the diesel engines. With their gleaming steel finish and metal and plastic interiors they seemed starker and colder than the dusty and often smelly carriages of the recent past. Also, there was no longer any opportunity of boarding a secret compartment unreachable from any other part of the train. What larks the boys had got up to sometimes on those occasions!

There had been games of pass the bag, dangling someone's satchel or item of clothing precariously out of the window and passing it along to the next compartment. It had to be swung to counteract the slipstream. More than one object went astray by that method.

Worse was the wilful damage caused by over exuberant youths who were even known to hack off the leather window straps or sections of the luggage rack webbing. Fittings were unscrewed or loosened.

These acts were only perpetrated by those who were safe in the knowledge that their crimes would be unwitnessed. Once off the trains and in the public eye, they reverted to almost normal and model citizens. No one would dare commit any deed that might be reportable to parents.

Truancy was unknown, at least at St Mary's. The only non-genuine absences were down to realistically feigned illness. Thus, on most days the same youthful faces gathered on platforms to await transportation to the destinations of their daily drudgery.

Apart from arrival at one's home station after a long school day, highlights to brighten up the mood were the times when passengers boarded and alighted. More specifically, when the girls from Accrington Grammar and the Convent hove in to view.

Despite ribald comments and gestures to suggest that the boys found the presence of the girls amusing, and the feigned indifference of the girls, most of the youths of both sexes nurtured a secret affection for one particular member of the opposite gender.

The handsomest boys were inevitably drawn to the prettiest girls and vice versa. Some more astute ones recognised other qualities beyond facial attraction. It seemed that personality was at least an equal draw. Thus the more bold and confident of the boys were able to successfully date the girl of their choice. That is, if they bothered, because they could always take their pick of girls in their local neighbourhoods, or so it seemed.

The girls, for their part, seemed content to endure the attention or otherwise of their counterparts. They took no lead in the matter of making a first move towards acquaintance.

In truth, the initial indicator was always the reaction of a girl to any overt sign of interest. By age-old custom, the use to which a female could put a glance or a smile, however slight, would be the key to any further friendship.

This would only pertain if the recipient of such indicators was bold enough to take the matter further.

So it was that many a young lad like Tommy and many a shy girl would spend frustrating months pondering and dreaming of what might be. There were other pursuits and distractions to occupy the energies of ardent youths.

Football was a great example of an alternative pursuit, at least for most boys. An exciting new horizon seemed to beckon for followers of the beautiful game. Wolverhampton Wanderers were one of the first English clubs to venture into the exotic world of Europe. Their management had imaginatively organised friendly games against continental opposition whose names and origins were shrouded in mystery and intrigue. Hitherto unheard of teams, the likes of which whet the appetites of the home fans, began to grace Molineux. Honved, Red Star Belgrade and Moscow Spartak – these were names that rolled off the tongue of football lovers across the land, even if most of them were only aware of such via the radio waves.

The Munich air disaster would throw a cloud over this bright new vision but even this tragedy gave way to a burgeoning fascination with the pan-European game. The magical team of Real Madrid began an era of domination in the competitive arena.

Popular music also began to exert an influence for the first time on the growing teens. Having lived on a diet of Alma Cogan, Dickie Valentine and Pat Boone, artists who were unlikely to stir the blood of adolescents, the teenagers of the late Fifties were about to have unleashed upon them a massive surge of energy.

The first that Tommy was aware of this was on a return trip from a visit to his grandma. Dad was negotiating the evening traffic through the centre of Preston when Shirley excitedly yelled out and pointed at a cinema that they were passing. Above the line of fans patiently queuing for admission was the huge billboard bearing, in giant letters, the legend "Elvis Presley starring in—". The rest was lost in the raindrops adorning the car's rear window.

Tommy was nonplussed by his sister's reaction but was tickled at Dad's nickname: "Hey, Elvis the Pelvis, how about that!"

Equally absorbing for Tommy was the brief glimpse of lads dressed in impossibly long jackets accompanied by girls with short and wide skirts which stood out from their legs, seemingly supported by an abundance of underskirt.

This new world of fashion and pursuit bore little resemblance to, and had little affect upon, the "real" world of the travelling schoolchildren. At least for the time being.

School terms came and went. With them arrived the inevitable internal tests and the ever increasing burden of homework. Although he didn't at the time fully realise the impact of this diet, Tommy was becoming ever more distanced from the world being experienced by his former chums. Some of them were by now beginning to contemplate the future beyond their pointless schooldays. There was talk of apprenticeships, pupils comparing notes on the fates of their elder brothers and sisters and their own work prospects.

Tommy could not see beyond the academic environment. School meant examinations and the possibility of further school, perhaps even more education beyond school as Shirley seemed to be aiming for. Life at St Mary's comprised learning for learning's sake.

In truth, Tommy's world was beginning to stifle him. The enrichment of a grammar school education was being counterbalanced by a suppression of life's hard knocks – a cocoon to enfold the maturing being.

At least his other school friends were undergoing the same process. This helped to dull Tommy's awareness of his situation, apart from the times spent at home away from this company.

By now something of a loner in his spare time, Tommy's dearest possession was his football. He would take himself off whenever time allowed to the Hard Platts with ball tucked underneath his arm. There, on the rolling hillside, he would spend hours dribbling and kicking the ball. There were wood and concrete benches (goalposts to Tommy) at which he would hone his shooting and trapping skills, endlessly blasting the ball at the wooden slats and controlling the rebounds.

He would still occasionally share the odd happy after-noon with Eric. They still met up to compare notes on their vastly differing school experiences. Eric's secondary modern contained girls for a start, which fact alone set it apart from life at St Mary's. They even indulged in residential school trips abroad.

Tommy was fascinated by Eric's account of his school's trip to Belgium, and of the antics they managed to engage in. The furthest afield that Tommy's class had ventured was Arnside on the North Lancashire coast, and that was two years ago. Not that there was anything to do when they got there, even in the unlikelihood that their teachers would grant permission or sufficient rein to their enthusiasm.

Luckily for Tommy, the Calverts did possess a car, unlike many of his neighbours. Not only that, it was exchanged for a newer model every few years. The Calvert omnibus clocked up a hefty mileage. Though it idled in the garage during the week as Father and Mother were able to walk to their factory and mill, it came out of hibernation every weekend. Not just for a wash and polish, as several other car-owners seemed to use their vehicles for, but actually to venture out on regular forays, at least in the summer months. This meant from March to October as far as Mr Calvert was concerned.

The big drive was still the annual cross-country safari during the Wakes fortnight. This almost inevitably meant their favourite West Country. No venue was visited twice. None of the Calverts could fathom the obsession of some of their neighbours with revisiting the same holiday resort year after year. No, they preferred new experiences, even if this sometimes resulted in disappointments compared to previous years. This meant that Tommy knew far more of England's green and pleasant land than most of his acquaintances, who seemed to be experts on North Wales, the Isle of Man or anywhere where there was a Butlin's or Pontin's, but ignorant of the rest of the realm.

Although Mr and Mrs Calvert's efforts throughout the year were focused on saving up for the annual adventure they still availed themselves of every opportunity to explore afield whenever the weather allowed.

The beauty of having a car was that they could travel to parts beyond the reach of rail links or coach routes – in fact any road which could accommodate their car, and even a few which shouldn't have.

Thus Tommy got to know places unheard of by the local boys and girls. He began to store up fond memories of locations such as Bolton Abbey, Malham, Stainforth and Howarth. He relished picnics on Clapham Common, en route to purchase damsons from Kendal. Mrs Calvert made this a compulsory pilgrimage so that she could make and bottle jars of home-made jam to last the year.

Dad had become the secretary of the local football club. This meant that Saturday afternoons were spent literally following the fortunes of the team. Their presence in the Lancashire Combination meant journeys on alternate Saturdays to venues such as Chorley, Lancaster, Skelmersdale and Prescot.

Tommy became a well known and liked figure at the matches. He was almost as close to the players as he had been to the lads of the works team, even though present company was a little more exalted.

His was still very much a male-dominated world. Female company was mostly restricted to his big sister Shirley. She was still on a different planet from him, though obviously they did have to endure each other's company.

Actually, Shirley was mellowing as she grew up. She seemed to be more immune from the nuisance of her younger brother. Now and again, she even exhibited flashes of concern for his well-being.

There was the occasion when she took Tommy down town and treated him to an ice cream sundae at Oddie's

Café, even allowing him seconds. This, of course, proved that she really cared for her brother, even though she shared nothing in common with him apart from having to occupy the same rear seat on car journeys.

For his part, Tommy had become rather less of an irritation to his sister. He had grown beyond the habit of doing things just to wind her up. He even tolerated her female friends without resorting to disgusting or insulting behaviour, limiting his teasing to good-humoured banter. They were both growing up.

New Relationships

S hirley had left secondary school and, having achieved the necessary grades at GCE "A" level, had moved on to college. She was going to train to become a teacher. Obviously the years spent enduring the antics of a younger brother had not put her off children altogether. On the contrary, they had probably helped to prepare her for the worst that young tykes could offer.

Tommy was now seriously embarked upon the road to his own external examinations. He still had no clear idea of what future road to take in life; it was sufficient to cope with the present. There were subjects which caused him concern as he had no particular affinity with them due to a lack of expertise. These included the apparently all important mathematics as well as the sciences – oh, and art and music as well. On the other hand, he was quite comfortable with English, modern languages and geography. His affection for the latter was down to a combination of his fascination with the world (credit to Mr and Mrs C for their peregrinations) and his liking for the affable Mr Whelan, who had been Tommy's geography master for most of his secondary years. He had actually managed to imbue the subject with a mystique and fascination that appealed to Tommy.

Homework became ever more demanding. It intruded upon his spare time to such a degree that only weekends afforded a release from the rigours of desk-bound study. During the week, time at home was compressed into a three-hour slot from the time Tommy arrived and ate his evening meal to bedtime. Into this gap he had to sandwich homework and television viewing. On light summer evenings he might manage an hour outside, but by that time many of his friends had made other plans.

There was only one thing for it; he simply had to do more of his homework on the train ride home. He even managed to fit in a few precious minutes' scribbling whilst perched on the platform bench awaiting the arrival of his train. Sadly, this only exacerbated the problem regarding social fulfilment. While other less responsible schoolmates enjoyed horseplay and occasional flirting with their Convent counterparts, Tommy began to be regarded as a killjoy at least.

This was hurtful to realise. No one enjoyed larking about more than Tommy. Hadn't he received more than his share of beatings from the school staff for his antics? Wasn't he the one who generally started the impromptu games of rugby in the train compartments, using his school cap as the ball? Didn't he entertain his chums with hilarious take-offs of the adults they encountered?

Now and again Tommy would break free of the shackles that his growing reputation seemed to attract. On these occasions his behaviour would verge on the extreme. This had the effect of making him more remote from the mainstream of his peers. Combined with his innate shyness – at least as far as the fair sex was concerned – it resulted in his marginalisation during times of mixed group gatherings.

Had he but known it, the same effect was becoming apparent elsewhere. There was someone else who, for slightly different reasons, was a kindred spirit. This person would begin to feature in Tommy's life and be the catalyst for his salvation…

In the meantime, Tommy's habit of unconsciously withdrawing from his fellow travellers in order to tackle his homework only attracted more bother. There was a small group of younger pupils who decided to amuse themselves at his expense. Whenever they caught Tommy engrossed in his books, they set out to tease and taunt him. They met with success. At first he endeavoured to ignore them; eventually, however, he would rise to their bait.

On one such occasion, he had taken shelter from the winter cold in the cavernous, high ceilinged waiting room on the main station platform. Pulling his briefcase onto his knees to use it as a desk, he opened his text and exercise books and began to work on the set task.

The three Convent girls – Jean, Hazel and Katherine, and a fourth one called Penny Conway – had also sought the warmth of the waiting room with its glowing coal fire. They were seated on the bench at the far side of the room and so Tommy could politely ignore them while he concentrated. That is, until the little terrors chose that moment to liven things up.

"Hey, it's Tommy the swot!" one of them called out as they stood by the partly open door.

After a brief glance up, Tommy decided to pretend that he hadn't heard. Just a few moments later, a bump on the window behind him was followed by the sight of one of the idiots. He must have been perched on the shoulders of his friend as he kept swaying about whilst pulling faces.

The girls looked across and giggled. Tommy reddened a little but stoically carried on. Then the door burst open once more. One of the group of tearaways had been propelled towards Tommy by his mates. Stumbling over Tommy's' feet, he recovered and gasped, "Swotty face!" before diving out of the door.

This was too much to bear. Tommy liked a good laugh himself, but not when he was the butt of the jocularity. Pushing aside his case, he leapt after the fleeing youth. Out of the waiting room and along the length of the platform the two figures raced. On the second lap of the platform buildings, Tommy caught up with his tormentor. Administering a couple of clips about the head, he extracted revenge.

On the walk back, he recovered his breath and some of his composure. Straightening his tie, he pushed open the waiting room door and returned to his books. A quick glance up confirmed that the girls were wreathed in smiles and had obviously enjoyed the entire episode. Several minutes later and they were still indulging in animated conversation and laughter. Tommy prayed with no great confidence that they weren't still amusing themselves at his expense.

When he dared to look across again after finishing his work, he noticed that one of the girls had a more sympathetic expression on her face. She was smiling, but not in a smug fashion. When Tommy's eyes met hers, she shyly averted her gaze. Tommy too became embarrassed, fiddling with the straps on his case. He was further distracted by a peculiar feeling of warmth which started in his chest and spread upwards through his shoulders to his face and ears. He felt sure that the rush of blood would manifest itself in a flush of redness, so he turned his head aside as far as he could.

Thankfully, the homeward train glided into the station and he was able to escape, joining the clamour for seats. As ever, the numerous groups of boys clustered together in their usual gatherings. Similarly, the girls, though fewer in number, also sought safety with their own kind. The effect of the single-sex education appeared to hold sway as long as the pupils were dressed in their uniforms and engaged in their schooling, which seemed to extend to travelling time.

Tommy did find company with several of his year group, and the one below, whilst en route. Another factor in social grouping was town of origin. Thus the Nelson lads tended to stick together, as did the Burnley and Colne crews. The mob from QEGS were a race apart anyway.

The group of four Convent girls were even more

divided. Katherine alighted at Burnley, Jean and Hazel a
Brierfield and only Penny carried on to Nelson. She was a
year younger anyway, although she had an older brother a
St Mary's. The two siblings would walk to and from the
station together, at which point each would then repair to
his or her companions.

On the walk home from the station was the time when
notes would be compared. Then the absent girls might
enter the conversation from time to time, vying with other
subjects of interest such as sport, hobbies and TV.

On this occasion, Steve mentioned to Peter that Jean had
been expressing interest. "Er, Peter, what do you think of
that Jean?"

"What? Why are you asking?" replied a surprised Peter.

"I don't know how to put this, but, er, her mates asked
me to ask you if you'll go out with her," was Steve's almost
apologetic answer.

All he got for his trouble was a look of disgust accompanied by a dismissive, "Humph!"

Tommy couldn't help but envy the handsome Peter who
could so emphatically turn down such an offer. Then again,
he could probably take his pick of admiring young girls near
where he lived. Mind you, even if he should ever be lucky
enough to receive such an invitation, Tommy was not at all
sure whether he would be courageous enough to take it up.

As the Nelsonian St Mary-ites met up on a daily basis,
they began to develop a growing friendship. The larger group,
which spanned three age ranges but did not include the
younger oiks, had a common interest in football. They
formed a team. They made arrangements to meet up on
Saturday mornings. The usual location was the pitches at the
top of the Hard Platts, next to the technical college grounds.

They didn't have a recognisable kit – each brought his
own gear to the games. It was decided that their official
colour would be white. The reasoning behind this was that

white was the easiest colour to replicate. Everyone apart from those lucky enough to possess a Real Madrid or Preston North End shirt could surely lay hands on a white tee shirt. Tommy was an exception.

When he rolled up to the pitch side on a clear autumnal morning, he tossed his duffle bag on the grass and unwound his boots from around his neck. Donning these and a pair of black shorts, he watched his mates girding themselves for action. They, in turn, looked to Tommy for him to complete his dressing.

"Where's your top?" enquired Steve.

"Haven't got one," was the reply.

"Then what are you going to play in?"

"This," revealed Tommy with a shrug.

So saying, he peeled off his jumper to expose a long sleeved nylon dress shirt. He then proceeded to roll up the sleeves tightly above elbow level. Without further thought he trotted onto the pitch and joined in the pre-match kick about. Everything was fine until a brief shower descended. It soaked everyone but its effect on Tommy was more dramatic. His best shirt, now saturated, clung to his body like a second skin. It also became transparent and showed the pinkness of the underlying flesh. As the brisk wind began to dry out the sodden players, it cut through Tommy like frozen needles. He was thus forced to run around the pitch even more frantically in an effort to bring back his circulation.

Eventually, a weary boy with glowing cheeks and runny nose arrived home to be chased off for a hot bath by Mrs Calvert.

Monday mornings witnessed an increasing aura of camaraderie surrounding the school-bound travellers. As well as the weekend's First and Second Division football results to trade insults about, there were their own playing exploits to mull over. The rival St Mary's and QEGS groups even found common ground for communication, if not actual friendship. Matches were arranged between them.

All this display of male comradeship impacted upon the amount of attention that could be devoted to other fellow passengers – to whit the Accrington Grammar and Convent girls. They still gravitated within their separate clusters. The boys seemed on the whole to be disinterested with their female counterparts, most preferring the company of girls from their own neighbourhoods with whom they could meet up in the evenings, homework permitting of course. Ah, homework, the great dampener on social interaction and free time!

Popular music became another major topic of interest. There were idols to be admired, home-grown as well as transatlantic. They were distant figures whose images were rarely seen unless one visited the cinema – a rare treat. They registered relatively little in the national press, but they could communicate via the airwaves. A few youths possessed record players. More usually they were the property of older brothers and sisters who jealously kept tight rein on them, hiding them and only bringing them out for use in order to repeatedly play their small collection of 45s.

Radios were a different matter. Most young lads and girls owned or had access to a portable set. Homework over, it became an increasingly popular ritual to retire to the bedroom, tune in to Radio Luxembourg or some other enlightened channel and be serenaded by Tommy Steele, Frankie Vaughan, Little Richard or, for the boys, Connie Francis or Rosemary Clooney.

Now, this was some common ground that could be shared by boys and girls alike. In fact, the vast majority of the songs encouraged fraternisation between the sexes. The singers crooned of love, found and lost, happiness and pain nd of a whole world that existed somewhere beyond the worries and trials of schooldays. Everyone could sing or hum a range of favourite hit tunes, even in the mind during an assembly or turgid maths lesson.

Saturday morning was now, for some, a case of strolling down to the town centre to look in on the record shops, browse through the disc collections and hear the latest releases belting out on the store's own record player. Tommy still preferred his football.

Happiness at Last

M r Calvert still enjoyed his hard work in the voluntary spare-time post of secretary to Nelson Football Club. His dedication and attention to detail, which was demonstrated in his working capacity at Victory V, made him an eminently suitable person for this role. It had been the appointment of Joe Fagan, a fellow Liverpudlian, as the Nelson manager which had first drawn him to the club. Now it was his second love. Attending every home game and travelling to most away games under his own steam, Mr Calvert became a club fixture. He often persuaded Tommy to accompany him (an easy task) whenever the lad wasn't playing himself.

One – in fact the only – perk of the job of club secretary was the availability of Cup Final tickets. Like every other affiliated club in the land, Nelson FC were allocated tickets for the most prestigious match of the season – the FA Cup Final. Most of the officials connected with the club were not too enamoured with the possibility of attending Wembley for the game, partly because they were not fans of either of the clubs involved, they perhaps didn't own a car and they weren't keen on the idea of undertaking such a long journey.

Fortunately for Tommy, these factors didn't count for much with his dad. Mr Calvert was a true football lover who would turn up to watch a gang of kids playing with a bladder. He *did* own a car and he had become used to travelling the length and breadth of England, admittedly in order to transport the family to their holiday destination. So it was that Mr C was able to lay his hands on a couple of much sought after tickets for the great occasion.

So, Tommy would actually be visiting the home of football, the national sporting shrine of Wembley Stadium. The occasion was the Cup Final between Nottingham Forest and Luton Town. This was yet another north v south clash. Forest were deemed to be a northern team, if only because they were nearer to Lancashire than their opponents. Besides, they played in red, the colour of the Calverts' home-town team.

Tommy and Dad travelled the long road south in the family Triumph Renown. They even passed through the centre of Luton, where Tommy was fascinated to see the shops and houses bedecked in team favours. Shop windows and lampposts alike were festooned with straw boaters, the eponymous "hatters" which were both the emblem and the nickname of the club.

Having been thrilled to watch several Cup Finals on black and white TV screens, usually those of kindly neighbours, Tommy was spellbound to now be a part of this tremendous ceremonial occasion. The images of the day would remain with him for ever. The walk up Wembley Way, the excited groups of rival supporters with their contrasting colours, the raucous touts eager to make a killing and, best of all, the sight of the famous white-clad figure leading the community singing from his tiny bandstand.

Even the match was decided in their favour. Forest won 2–1, despite losing a player with a broken leg and being reduced to playing with ten men. No amount of Cup Finals seen played out on bright grey screens could compare with the splendour of the actual event in living and breathing colour and noise. One day Tommy's own team, Liverpool, would tread the hallowed turf in successful pursuit of the glittering silver trophy. Of that, he was utterly convinced.

Tommy fell asleep during the lengthy drive north long before Dad pulled up on the backstreet outside the family home. What an experience he would have to relate to his jealous school pals! He was even looking forward to going back to school on Monday morning.

And so, football continued to occupy most of Tommy's attention and energy. He could happily endure the gloating of the Clarets' fans – most of his travelling companions – and the Rovers' fans – many of his school friends – in the firm belief that his own Liverpool team were a superior outfit even though they still languished in the Second Division.

What Tommy found increasingly hard to bear was the apparent success of a growing number of his peers in developing friendships with girls. Quite a few were actually dating a particular person while others appeared to be able to enjoy the company of several girls in turn. One or two were even cultivating relationships with the girls on the train, though they had to endure the taunts of their friends for their pains.

In this matter, Tommy was far too reserved. He would gaze from a distance, often through a carriage window, at the girls as if at a shop window peering in at objects beyond his reach. In his case, it was lack of confidence rather than cash which restricted him to the role of spectator.

It didn't help matters when he witnessed his elder sister preparing to go out at weekends. She would spend inordinate amounts of time in her bedroom, during which she would give Tommy short shrift if he dared to venture within her space. Ostensibly, she was going to meet up with her friend Kathleen, but judging by the meticulous effort taken over her appearance, there were going to be boys involved somewhere in the process.

Tommy began to imagine what it might be about these boys which would attract his sister. Could he learn anything?

"Where are you going?" he ventured.

"Mind your own business," retorted Shirley, "and get out of my room and leave me alone!"

"Are you meeting anyone else?" from the landing.

"I've told you!" cried Shirley, hurling a hairbrush at his retreating figure.

Oh well, so much for that idea. Perhaps he could follow her and see what she and Kathleen got up to? This thought was dismissed almost as soon as it arrived. Far too dangerous a ploy. Anyway, how could he get past Mum and Dad at the same time as his sister left the house? Someone would smell a rat.

Tommy decided that he would pump his friends for information – surreptitiously of course – by initiating the most innocent of conversations.

The first opportunity arose when he heard Steve talking about his previous weekend's activities, including a date with his girlfriend, Christine.

"How come you ended up going out with her?" Tommy asked, as innocently as he could.

"It was her friend. She asked me if I wanted to go out with her so I said OK," was the unhelpful if truthful reply. Lucky old Steve.

On many occasions over the following weeks Tommy played out in his mind several ideal scenarios. The boldest of these involved him walking up to one of the girls (he had a good idea which one) and asking her straight out to go out with him. This involved two difficulties. He would first of all need the rare opportunity of being alone with the ideal person, and secondly the courage to act promptly given the chance. He knew he wouldn't be able to pull it off.

That left the only other realistic chance. One of his intended's friends would have to take the lead, on her behalf, and ask Tommy the same question that lucky old Steve had been asked. How did he even know that the person he desired felt that way about him, sufficiently to take the initiative?

Thus Tommy remained unfulfilled in his desire for female companionship for the time being.

It was while talking to Eric that Tommy first began to think about life beyond his schooldays. The two of them were trudging the local streets, Eric lugging a large canvas bag. He had obtained a job at Old Atkin's shop, delivering the evening papers. Tommy was able to join his friend and offer assistance because St Mary's half-term break differed from the local school's.

Eric explained that he had taken on the job to save up for his holidays. He had even opened a post office account so that a little money could be put by for the future. At school the teachers had begun careers talks with the older pupils and urged them to consider a trade. Eric said that he wanted to be a joiner. Tommy hadn't given any thought to the possibility of taking on full-time employment. His sister was going to leave school and go on to college for goodness knows how many more years. Presumably he would do the same, at least going on to sixth form.

Even more amazingly, Tommy had actually heard Brian and the other lads discussing one night outside the chippy their plans for when they left school. These included not only finding steady employment but meeting up with a girl, marrying and settling down in a house of their own! The more sensible ones, though, talked of a life of freedom, of being single and travelling the country, perhaps even abroad.

Ideally, Tommy dreamed of the perfect combination: to meet a girl with whom one could find mutual attraction and interest and to pursue shared dreams without the burden of any responsibilities. Did anyone manage to achieve this?

The end of Tommy's tortured days of discontent was to come sooner rather than later.

After trudging up the ramp leading to Platform 4 and the train home after a particularly weary autumn term day at school, he slumped on a bench and placed his school bag on the floor between his knees. Gazing along the length of the station, he spotted the usual sight of the three Convent schoolgirls huddled together.

This time he allowed his gaze to linger on the scene for several seconds, oblivious to other pupils and adults scattered around. So engrossed was he that he was caught unawares. The girls had paused briefly in their conversation. Katherine happened to glance in his general direction.

Had she seen him looking at them? He hoped not. Quickly he averted his eyes and focused on some pigeons flapping about in the roof space. He risked a furtive dart back in their direction.

Katherine, thus also caught out, turned back to her friends. Had that been a slight smile on her face before she turned away? Probably not. Either he had imagined it or something else had amused her. Maybe – maybe not.

Wishful thinking on Tommy's part was swept away by the gliding in of the diesel train and the flashing of the windows, reflecting the dim platform lamplights. He pulled open a compartment door and stepped aboard. This time he did not seek out the company of his mates. The carriage was one of the ones with a central aisle and table seats along both sides.

Tommy strode purposefully towards the rear of the train, holding his head high. He deliberately avoided looking at the other lads and managed to ignore all comments and exhortations. Reaching his goal, he flung his bag on the table and slid into a window seat.

As the train jerked in to motion, Tommy gazed out at the dimming sky, made even darker by the high walls and roof of the station. What he saw was a pensive and furrowed visage staring back at him. He attempted a smile at himself and then stared unseeingly at the townscape rushing past the window. Just briefly, he thought about the other homeward-bound pupils on the same journey. Where exactly on the train were they? What would they be doing now?

Accrington came and went. Huncoat and Hapton passed by. Next stop was Rosegrove. Gradually the population of the train begin to thin. After the marshalling yards at Rosegrove the train's next stop would be Burnley Central. Tommy came to a decision.

As soon as the train squealed to a halt at Burnley, he was standing in the corridor close to a door clutching his bag. Pressing his face up to the glass, he noted the passengers alighting from the train. They were the usual ones.

Leaving it as late as possible, Tommy took a deep breath and gave a final fleeting thought as to how he would get home. Then he pressed down the brass handle, flung open the door and skipped onto the platform.

No one seemed to have witnessed his peculiar action. He hurried to lose himself in the exiting throng, having seen Katherine's distinctive school hat and figure ahead of him. He closed the gap whilst trying to maintain a secretive presence.

When the cluster of people had emerged onto the street, Katherine glanced around before heading off for home. Seeing Tommy approach, closer than he had intended, she exclaimed in surprise, "Hello, what are you doing here?"

"Er, I have to get something from Burnley before I go home," Tommy replied unconvincingly.

"Oh, right," smiled Katherine.

Did a faint expression of disbelief flicker across her face, or had Tommy imagined it in his confused state? Has she sussed me out? he thought in a sudden attack of panic, What must she be thinking about me? Does she think I'm an idiot?

His worries on this score proved groundless as she turned away to continue homeward. This only served to bring him to near panic. Had he left himself stranded from

his means of getting home, and gone to this supreme effort
at risk of his reputation, all for nothing? A little voice urged
him to do something for goodness' sake.

So he somehow found the courage and the voice to blurt
out, "Er, can I, er, carry your bag for you?" He managed to
get it out while his face began to turn a deepening red.

To Katherine's great credit, she managed to stifle the
urge to appear shocked and to rebuff the pass. To his great
surprise and delight the response was a smile and a chirpy,
"OK then," as she passed him the straps of her schoolbag.

Had he but known how close was the call, Tommy
would surely have fainted from the tension. Even now, he
was almost a helpless bag of nerves. It took him two goes to
get a firm grip on Katherine's schoolbag. No sooner had he
begun to recover his composure than he faced his next test.

"Didn't you say you had to get some shopping?" asked a
concerned Katherine. They were heading away from the
town centre.

"Oh, it's all right. I'll do that afterwards," replied
Tommy as nonchalantly as he could, knowing full well that
they were both aware that the shops would be closed by the
time he retraced his steps.

Katherine attempted to relieve the tension. "Have you
got much homework to do tonight?"

"Not too much," responded Tommy. Realising that he
had to keep the momentum going he added, "How about
you? What kind of day have you had?"

"All right, really. The worst bit was when we had Sister
Imelda. She takes us for French and she's horrible. Anyway,
she didn't give us any homework for a change."

The couple lapsed into silence. Each was blissfully happy
in their shared company but also shy and ill at ease, not
knowing what to say or do next. Tommy was sure that he
felt worse. Wasn't it the boys who were always expected to
take the lead in such matters? What should he say next?

How could he change the atmosphere from one of polite ness and platonic acquaintance to one where he could giv vent to his true feelings?

Before they were ready, the couple found themselve entering the street where Katherine lived. They paused a the corner. She took back her bag with a genuine expressio of gratitude.

Tommy, with a sudden inspirational spurt of recklessness reached out and took an ever so gentle and tentative clasp o her fingertips with both hands. "Can I see you again?" h asked limply and rather inadequately. Of course they woul be able to see each other every day on the train.

"Yes, sure," breathed Katherine, more confidently than she felt.

Tommy's heart was pumping madly by now. Again, a little voice told him that he needed to say more.

"What about Saturday? Can I take you to the pictures?" he pleaded.

"I think so," replied Katherine, then, realising that she needed to add more, "Yes, OK. What time?"

This caught Tommy completely off guard. How could he arrange it? How to get out of the house? What excuse could he give? All these thoughts rushed through his mind in a twinkling. "How about six o'clock?" he managed.

"Fine. Where shall we meet?"

"Er, I dunno. What about at the end of your street by the main road?"

"Are you sure you'll be able to find it again?" she smiled.

"Course I will."

"All right then. It's a date," was Katherine's final and delightful response.

Though their hands had dropped to their sides, they were both still clutching each other's. As she let go and turned to head for home, Katherine's lips brushed fleetingly across Tommy's hot cheek.

She hurried away in her embarrassment. He gazed after

her in bliss and rapture. He continued to stare at her receding figure until she reached her front door and turned towards him. With an encouraging wave, she stepped up to her threshold. Tommy vigorously returned the gesture. He carried on staring after her until she disappeared inside her house.

He had little recollection of his journey home. His footsteps floated on air and transported him first to the bus stop for Nelson and then on the walk up Lomeshaye Road to home. He began to invent his story to explain his late arrival...

Printed in the United Kingdom
by Lightning Source UK Ltd.
112211UKS00001B/4-51